A VISIT TO THE ULTIMATE FAT FARM...

and other events and places terrifying, bizarre, hilarious, amazing and amusing, from one of the most celebrated writers of imaginative fiction of our time.

Other Stories And:
THE ATTACK OF THE GIANT BABY

KIT REED
author of
MAGIC TIME

Berkley books by Kit Reed

MAGIC TIME
OTHER STORIES AND: THE ATTACK OF THE GIANT BABY

Also by Kit Reed

MOTHER ISN'T DEAD SHE'S ONLY SLEEPING
AT WAR AS CHILDREN
THE BETTER PART
CRY OF THE DAUGHTER
TIGER RAG
CAPTAIN GROWNUP
THE BALLAD OF T. RANTULA

THE ATTACK of the GIANT BABY
Other Stories and...

KIT REED

BERKLEY BOOKS, NEW YORK

Some of these stories have been previously published in Great Britain by Victor Gollancz Ltd in the book KILLER MICE.

OTHER STORIES AND:
THE ATTACK OF
THE GIANT BABY

A Berkley Book / published by arrangement with
the author

PRINTING HISTORY
Berkley edition / August 1981

All rights reserved.
Copyright © 1981 by Kit Reed.
WINTER from *Winter's Tales*. Copyright © 1969 by Kit Reed.
THE VINE from *The Magazine of Fantasy and Science Fiction*
Copyright © 1967 by Kit Reed.
WINSTON from *Orbit 5* copyright © 1969 by Kit Reed.
THE FOOD FARM from *Orbit 2* copyright © 1974 by Kit Reed.
SONGS OF WAR From *Nova 4* copyright © 1974 by Kit Reed.
PILOTS OF THE PURPLE TWILIGHT
copyright © 1981 by Kit Reed.
THE THING AT WEDGERLEY copyright © 1976 by Kit Reed.
GRAN from *Argosy*, London copyright © 1970 by Kit Reed.
DEATH OF A MONSTER copyright © 1970 by Kit Reed.
CYNOSURE from *The Magazine of Fantasy and Science Fiction*
copyright © 1964 by Kit Reed.
ACROSS THE BAR from *Orbit 9* copyright © 1971 by Kit Reed.
EMPTY NEST from *The Magazine of Fantasy and Science Fiction*.
copyright © 1959 by Kit Reed.
IN BEHALF OF THE PRODUCT from *Bad Moon Rising*
copyright © 1973 by Kit Reed.
THE ATTACK OF THE GIANT BABY
copyright © 1975 by Kit Reed.
THE WANDERING GENTILE copyright © 1976 by Kit Reed.
MOON copyright © 1981 by Kit Reed.
Cover illustration by Jill Bauman.
This book may not be reproduced in whole or in part,
by mimeograph or any other means, without permission.
For information address: Berkley Publishing Corporation,
200 Madison Avenue, New York, New York 10016.

ISBN: 0-425-05032-7

A BERKLEY BOOK ® TM 757, 375

PRINTED IN THE UNITED STATES OF AMERICA

Other Stories and...

THE ATTACK OF THE GIANT BABY

KIT REED

BERKLEY BOOKS, NEW YORK

Some of these stories have been previously published in Great Britain
by Victor Gollancz Ltd in the book KILLER MICE.

OTHER STORIES AND:
THE ATTACK OF
THE GIANT BABY

A Berkley Book / published by arrangement with
the author

PRINTING HISTORY
Berkley edition / August 1981

All rights reserved.
Copyright © 1981 by Kit Reed.
WINTER from *Winter's Tales*. Copyright © 1969 by Kit Reed.
THE VINE from *The Magazine of Fantasy and Science Fiction*
Copyright © 1967 by Kit Reed.
WINSTON from *Orbit 5* copyright © 1969 by Kit Reed.
THE FOOD FARM from *Orbit 2* copyright © 1974 by Kit Reed.
SONGS OF WAR From *Nova 4* copyright © 1974 by Kit Reed.
PILOTS OF THE PURPLE TWILIGHT
copyright © 1981 by Kit Reed.
THE THING AT WEDGERLEY copyright © 1976 by Kit Reed.
GRAN from *Argosy*, London copyright © 1970 by Kit Reed.
DEATH OF A MONSTER copyright © 1970 by Kit Reed.
CYNOSURE from *The Magazine of Fantasy and Science Fiction*
copyright © 1964 by Kit Reed.
ACROSS THE BAR from *Orbit 9* copyright © 1971 by Kit Reed.
EMPTY NEST from *The Magazine of Fantasy and Science Fiction*.
copyright © 1959 by Kit Reed.
IN BEHALF OF THE PRODUCT from *Bad Moon Rising*
copyright © 1973 by Kit Reed.
THE ATTACK OF THE GIANT BABY
copyright © 1975 by Kit Reed.
THE WANDERING GENTILE copyright © 1976 by Kit Reed.
MOON copyright © 1981 by Kit Reed.
Cover illustration by Jill Bauman.
This book may not be reproduced in whole or in part,
by mimeograph or any other means, without permission.
For information address: Berkley Publishing Corporation,
200 Madison Avenue, New York, New York 10016.

ISBN: 0-425-05032-7

A BERKLEY BOOK ® TM 757, 375

PRINTED IN THE UNITED STATES OF AMERICA

to remember Tony Boucher

Contents

Winter *1*
The Vine *11*
Winston *24*
The Food Farm *38*
Songs of War *50*
Pilots of the Purple Twilight *96*
The Thing at Wedgerley *109*
Gran *115*
Death of a Monster *124*
Cynosure *134*
Across the Bar *146*
Empty Nest *157*
In Behalf of the Product *168*
The Attack of the Giant Baby *178*
The Wandering Gentile *187*
Moon *199*

Winter

It was late fall when he come to us, there was a scum of ice on all the puddles and I could feel the winter cold and fearsome in my bones, the hunger inside me was already uncurling, it would pace through the first of the year but by spring it would be raging like a tiger, consuming me until the thaw when Maude could hunt again and we would get the truck down the road to town. I was done canning but I got the tomatoes we had hanging in the cellar and I canned some more; Maude went out and brought back every piece of meat she could shoot and all the grain and flour and powdered milk she could bring in one truckload, we had to lay in everything we could before the snow could come and seal us in. The week he come Maude found a jack-rabbit stone dead in the road, it was frozen with its feet sticking straight up, and all the meat hanging in the cold-room had froze. Friday there was rime on the grass and when I looked out I seen footprints in the rime, I said Maude, someone is in the playhouse and we went out and there he was. He was asleep in the mess of clothes we always dressed up in, he had his head on the velvet gown my mother wore to the Exposition and his feet on the satin gown she married Father in, he had pulled her feather boa around his neck and her fox fur was wrapped around his loins.

Before he come, Maude and me would pass the winter talking about how it used to be, we would call up the past between us and look at it and Maude would end by blaming me. I could of married either Lister Hoffman or Harry Mead and left this place for good if it hadn't been for you, Lizzie. I'd tell her, Hell, I never needed you. You didn't marry them because you didn't marry them, you was scared of it and you would use me for an excuse. She would get mad then. It's a lie. Have it your way, I would tell her, just to keep the peace.

We both knew I would of married the first man that asked me, but nobody would, not even with all my money, nobody would ask me because of the taint. If nobody had of known then some man might of married me, but I went down to the field with Miles Harrison once while Father was still alive, and Miles and me, we almost, except that the blackness took me, right there in front of him, and so I never did. Nobody needed to know, but then Miles saw me fall down in the field. I guess it was him that put something between my teeth, but when I come to myself he was gone. Next time I went to town they all looked at me funny, some of them would try and face up to me and be polite but they was all jumpy, thinking would I do it right there in front of them, would I froth much, would they be hurt, as soon as was decent they would say Excuse me, I got to, anything to get out of there fast. When I run into Miles that day he wouldn't look at me and there hasn't been a man near me since then, not in more than fifty years, but Miles and me, we almost, and I have never stopped thinking about that.

Now Father is gone and my mother is gone and even Lister Hoffman and Miles Harrison and half the town kids that used to laugh at me, they are all gone, but Maude still reproaches me, we sit after supper and she says If it hadn't been for you I would have grandchildren now and I tell her I would have had them before ever she did because she never liked men, she would only suffer them to get children and that would be too much trouble, it would hurt. That's a lie, Lizzie, she would say. Harry and me used to . . . and I would tell her You never, but Miles and me . . . Then we would both think about being young and having people's hands on us but memory turns Maude bitter and she can never leave it at that, she says, It's all your fault, but I know in my heart that people make their lives what they want them, and all she ever wanted was to be locked in here with nobody to make demands on her, she wanted to stay in this house with me, her dried-up sister, cold and safe, and if the hunger is on her, it has come on her late.

After a while we would start to make up stuff: Once I went with a boy all the way to Portland . . . Once I danced all night and half the morning, he wanted to kiss me on the place where my elbow bends . . . We would try to spin out the winter but even that was not enough and so we would always be left with the hunger; no matter how much we laid in, the meat was always gone before the thaw and I suppose it was really our lives we was judging but we would decide nothing in the cans looked good to us and so we would sit and dream and hunger and wonder if we would die of it, but finally the thaw would come and Maude would look at me and sigh: If only we had another chance.

Well now perhaps we will.

We found him in the playhouse, maybe it was seeing him asleep in the middle of my mother's clothes or maybe it was being in the playhouse, where we pretended so many times, but there was this boy, or man, and something about him called up our best memories, there was promise wrote all over him. I am too old, I am all dried out, but I have never stopped thinking about that one time and seeing that boy there, I could pretend he was Miles and I was still young. I guess he sensed us, he woke up fast and went into a crouch, maybe he had a knife, and then I guess he saw it was just two big old ladies in Army boots, he said, I run away from the Marines, I needed a place to sleep.

Maude said, I don't care what you need, you got to get out of here, but when he stood up he wobbled. His hair fell across his head like the hair on a boy I used to know and I said, Maude, why don't you say yes to something just this once.

He had on this denim shirt and pants like no uniform I ever seen and he was saying, Two things happened, I found out I might have to shoot somebody in the war and then I made a mistake and they beat me so I cut out of there. He smiled and he looked open. I stared hard at Maude and Maude finally looked at me and said, All right, come up to the house and get something to eat.

He said his name was Arnold but when we asked him Arnold what, he said Never mind. He was in the kitchen by then, he had his head bent over a bowl of oatmeal and some biscuits I had made, and when I looked at Maude she was watching the way the light slid across his hair. When we told him our names he said, You are both beautiful ladies, I could see Maude's hands go up to her face and she went into her room and when she come back I saw she had put color on her cheeks. While we was alone he said how good the biscuits was and wasn't that beautiful silver, did I keep it polished all myself and I said well yes, Maude brings in supplies but I am in charge of the house and making all the food. She come back then and saw us with our heads together and said to Arnold, I guess you'll be leaving soon.

I don't know, he said, they'll be out looking for me with guns and dogs.

That's no never mind of ours.

I never done nothing bad in the Marines, we just had different ideas. We both figured it was something worse but he looked so sad and tired and besides, it was nice to have him to talk to, he said, I just need a place to hole up for a while.

Maude said, You could always go back to your family.

He said, They never wanted me. They was always mean-hearted, not like you.

I took her aside and said, It wouldn't kill you to let him stay on, Maude, it's time we had a little life around here.

There won't be enough food for three.

He won't stay long. Besides, he can help you with the chores.

She was looking at his bright hair again, she said, like it was all my doing, If you want to let him stay I guess we can let him stay.

He was saying, I could work for my keep.

All right, I said, you can stay on until you get your strength.

My heart jumped. A man, I thought. A man. How can I explain it? It was like being young, having him around. I looked at Maude and saw some of the same things in her eyes, hunger and hope, and I thought, You are ours now, Arnold, you are all ours. We will feed you and take care of you and when you want to wander we will let you wander, but we will never let you go.

Just until things die down a little, he was saying.

Maude had a funny grin. Just until things die down.

Well it must of started snowing right after dark that afternoon, because when we all waked up the house was surrounded. I said, Good thing you got the meat in, Maude, and she looked out, it was still blowing snow and it showed no signs of stopping, she looked out and said, I guess it is.

He was still asleep, he slept the day through except he

stumbled down at dusk and dreamed over a bowl of my rabbit stew, I turned to the sink and when I looked back the stew was gone and the biscuits was gone and all the extra in the pot was gone, I had a little flash of fright, it was all disappearing too fast. Then Maude come over to me and hissed, The food, he's eating all the food and I looked at his brown hands and his tender neck and I said, It don't matter, Maude, he's young and strong and if we run short he can go out into the snow and hunt. When we looked around next time he was gone, he had dreamed his way through half a pie and gone right back to bed.

Next morning he was up before the light, we sat together around the kitchen table and I thought how nice it was to have a man in the house, I could look at him and imagine anything I wanted. Then he got up and said, Look, I want to thank you for everything, I got to get along now and I said, You can't, and he said, I got things to do, I been here long enough, but I told him You can't, and took him over to the window. The sun was up by then and there it was, snow almost to the window ledges, like we have every winter, and all the trees was shrouded, we could watch the sun take the snow and make it sparkle and I said, Beautiful snow, beautiful, and he only shrugged and said, I guess I'll have to wait till it clears off some. I touched his shoulder. I guess it will. I knew not to tell him it would never clear off, not until late spring; maybe he guessed, anyway he looked so sad I gave him Father's silver snuffbox to cheer him up.

He would divide his time between Maude and me, he played Rook with her and made her laugh so hard she gave him her pearl earrings and the brooch Father brought her back from Quebec. I gave him Grandfather's diamond stickpin because he admired it, and for Christmas we gave him the cameos and Father's gold-headed cane. Maude got the flu over New Year's and Arnold and me spent New Year's Eve together, I mulled some wine and he hung up some of Mama's jewelry from the center light, and touched it and made it twirl. We lit candles and played the radio, New Year's Eve in Times Square and somebody's Make-believe Ballroom, I went to pour another cup of wine and his hand was on mine on the bottle, I knew my lips was red for once and next day I gave him Papa's fur-lined coat.

I guess Maude suspected there was something between us, she looked pinched and mean when I went in with her broth at lunch, she said, Where were you at breakfast and I said, Maude, it's New Year's Day, I thought I would like to sleep in for once. She was quick and spiteful. You were with him. I thought, If she wants to think that about me, let her, and I let my eyes go sleepy and I said, We had to see the New Year in, didn't we? She was out of bed in two days, I have never seen anybody get up so fast after the flu. I think she couldn't stand us being where she couldn't see what we was up to every living minute. Then I got sick and I knew what torture it must have been for her, just laying there, I would call Maude and I would call her, and sometimes she would come and sometimes she wouldn't come and when she finally did look in on me I would say, Maude, where have you been and she would only giggle and not answer. There was meat cooking all the time, roasts and chops and chicken fricassee, when I said Maude, you're going to use it up, she would only smile and say, I just had to show him who's who in the kitchen, he tells me I'm a better cook than you ever was. After a while I got up, I had to even if I was dizzy and like to throw up, I had to get downstairs where I could keep an eye on them. As soon as I was up to it I made a roast of venison that would put hair on an egg and after that we would vie with each other in the kitchen, Maude and me. Once I had my hand on the skillet handle and she come over and tried to take it away, she was saying, Let me serve it up for him. I said, you're a fool, Maude, I cooked this and she hissed at me, through the steam, it won't do you no good, Lizzie, it's me he loves, and I just pushed her away and said, you goddam fool, he loves me, and I give him my amethysts just to prove it. A couple of days later I couldn't find neither of them nowhere, I thought I heard noises up in the back room and I went up there and if they was in there they wouldn't answer, the door was locked and they wouldn't say nothing, not even when I knocked and knocked and knocked. So the next day I took him up in my room and we locked the door and I told him a story about every piece in my jewel box, even the cheap ones, when Maude tapped and whined outside the door we would just shush, and when we did come out and she said, All right, Lizzie, what was you doing in there, I only giggled and wouldn't tell.

She shouldn't of done it, we was all sitting around the table after dinner and she looked at me hard and said, You know something, Arnold, I wouldn't get too close to Lizzie, she has fits. Arnold only tried to look like it didn't matter, but after Maude went to bed I went down to make sure it was all right. He was still in the kitchen, whittling, and when I tried to touch his hand he pulled away.

I said, Don't be scared, I only throw one in a blue moon.

He said, That don't matter.

Then what's the matter?

I don't know, Miss Lizzie, I just don't think you trust me.

Course I trust you, Arnold, don't I give you everything?

He just looked sad. Everything but trust.

I owe you so much, Arnold, you make me feel so young.

He just smiled for me then. You look younger, Miss Lizzie, you been getting younger every day I been here.

You did it.

If you let me, I could make you really young.

Yes, Arnold, yes.

But I have to know you trust me.

Yes, Arnold.

So I showed him where the money was. By then it was past midnight and we was both tired, he said, Tomorrow, and I let him go off to get his rest.

I don't know what roused us both and brought us out into the hall but I bumped into Maude at dawn, we was both standing in our nightgowns like two ghosts. We crept downstairs together and there was light in the kitchen, the place where we kept the money was open, empty, and there was a crack of light in the door to the cold room. I remember looking through and thinking, The meat is almost gone. Then we opened the door a crack wider and there he was, he had made a sledge, he must of sneaked down there and worked on it every night. It was piled with stuff, our stuff, and now he had the door to the outside open, he had dug himself a ramp out of the snow and he was lashing some home-made snowshoes on his feet, in another minute he would cut out of there.

When he heard us he turned.

I had the shotgun and Maude had the axe.

He said, You can have all your stuff.

We said, We don't care about the stuff, Arnold. How could we tell him it was our youth he was taking away?

He looked at us, wall-eyed. You can have it all, just let me out.

You said you loved us, Arnold.

He was scrabbling up the snow ramp. Never mind what I told you, let me out of here.

He was going to get away in another minute, so Maude let him have it with the axe.

Afterwards we closed the way to the outside and stood there and looked at each other, I couldn't say what was in my heart so I only looked at Maude, we was both sad, sad, I said, The food is almost gone.

Maude said, Everything is gone. We'll never make it to spring.

I said, We have to make it to spring.

Maude looked at him laying there. You know what he told me? He said, I can make you young.

Me too, I said. There was something in his eyes that made me believe it.

Maude's eyes was aglitter, she said, The food is almost gone.

I knew what she meant, he was going to make us young. I don't know how it will work in us, but he is going to make us young, it will be as if the fits had never took me, never in all them years. Maude was looking at me, waiting, and after a minute I looked square at her and I said, I know.

So we et him.

The Vine

Day in, day out, summer in, summer out, through fire, flood and contumely, over the centuries Baskin's family had tended the vine. No one knew precisely how old the vine was, or who had planted it and set the first Baskin to care for it; when the first settlers came to the valley, the vine was already there. No one knew who had built the immense conservatory which housed it, or who sent the trucks which came every autumn to take away the fruit.

The Baskins themselves didn't know; still they had cared for the vine from the beginning, pruning, shaping and harvesting, watering it in times when no one else had water, feeding it when there was no food. They lived in a small cottage in the shadow of the trunk, giving all their days to it; their backs were bent and their skins were pale and soft from a lifetime of hothouse air. When they died they were buried in the family plot just outside the giant conservatory, laid in the ground without shrouds or coffins so that they could go on feeding the vine. The eldest son was the only one who married. He usually did his courting outside the valley so that the bride would not know until he brought her home that she was to bear sons and daughters to care for the vine. Although there was no proof, there were rumors of a ritual bloodletting, in which the Baskins gave of themselves four times a year, enriching the earth at its base.

Even contained as it was within multifaceted glass walls, the vine overshadowed the entire valley. In the best times farmers could look at their finest fruit and know it could not measure up to the grapes hanging inside the conservatory. When frost came early or drought leached the soil, they blamed the vine. Yet even as they hated it, they were drawn by it. Summer and winter a steady procession came from the farthest corners of the valley and in time from the countryside beyond, all shuffling towards the great conservatory, waiting in silence until it was their turn to go inside.

Outside the conservatory, no grass grew. For hundreds of yards around the earth was barren, sapped. Visitors approached over a single elevated pathway, conscious of the immense, powerful network spreading just beneath their feet, the root system of the vine. Ahead, the conservatory would be dark with it, each glass pane filled with burgeoning leaves and heavy, importunate fruit. At the door they would give a coin to the youngest Baskin daughter and go through the turnstile, craning over the rail to look at the sinuous trunk. Their eyes would follow it to the base and the carefully turned earth which supported it, and most would refuse to comprehend that the thing measured twenty feet across. The earth was intersected by a series of wooden walks along which the Baskins went with shears and hoes and thongs, ready to soften a clod of earth or tie up any part of the plant which might free itself from the enormous arbor and begin to droop. Overhead the arbor spread, entwined and almost obscured by the many flexing, sinewy coils of the giant vine. The entire conservatory was filled by the branches and fruit of this single plant, so that the visitor could stand on the balcony, just to the left of the Baskins' cottage, and look out across yards and yards of open space intersected by walks and roofed in leafy green. From this green roof hung clump after identical clump of flawless grapes, the opulent purple fruit of the vine. Straining into the green gloom, the visitor could see the Baskins scurrying back and forth along the pathways, pale, incessant wraiths in faded chambray shirts. There were those who said the vine sucked the life out of the Baskins; there were others who said the Baskins took their life from the vine. Whatever the truth, the visitor would sense in their movements a haste, a frightening urgency, and in the next moment he might clutch at his throat as if the vine threatened him too, draining the air he breathed, and so he would turn hurriedly and flee into the sunshine, hardly noticing the others who pressed to the rail to take his place.

Even frightened, so, the visitor would return. In his own distant home in another season, he would close his eyes and see once again the brooding tracery. Something would draw him back, and so he would come again, perhaps with a bride or a firstborn son, saying: I tried to tell you; there are not enough words for the vine. So the crowds coming to the valley grew larger, and in time there had to be new roads and places to eat, and since some came from such distances that they needed to rest before going on, the valley people built inns. One by one the farmers cut down their own production, abandoning vineyards to put their money into restaurants and motels. Movie houses sprang up, and someone built a terrace overlooking the conservatory, dotting it with purple umbrellas and studding it with bathing pools. Someone created small, jeweled grape clusters for visitors to buy, and someone else bottled a wine which he told visitors came from the fruit of the vine. The people in the valley grew sleek and prospered, and although they still lived in the shadow of the vine, they no longer cursed it. Instead they would look at the sky and say: Hope it rains, the vine needs water. Or: If there's hail, I hope it doesn't break the glass and hurt the vine. In time they stopped farming altogether, and from that time on, their lives depended on the steady flow of visitors who came to see the vine.

So it was that Charles Baskin was born into a time of prosperity, and the people of the valley no longer shunned the Baskins. Instead they said: Is your family keeping busy? Or, slapping Charles on the shoulder: Hi, Charlie. How's the vine?

Fine, he would say—distractedly, because he was approaching his twenties: he was the first-born and it was time for him to find a wife. In the old days, it would have been more difficult—a Baskin who went courting in the old days had to take a cart or a wagon and go over the mountains, traveling until he came to a town where they had never heard of the vine.

Charles's own mother had come from such a town. She came with her eyes dazzled by love and her ears full of his father's lies and promises, understanding only when she entered the conservatory that she would spend the rest of her life caring for the vine. Charles had seen her languish all through his childhood, sitting down on a root to weep, and he had listened night after night to her tales of life outside. Yet in the scant twenty years since his birth the climate and temper of life in the valley had changed. His mother's parents came to visit, and instead of protesting, they were delighted. The mayor brought them in, bursting with pride, and the old man and the old woman admired the conservatory and exclaimed over the cottage and even went so far as to pat the trunk of the vine. She was still protesting, trying to explain when they said:

"You must be so happy, dear." And left.

Charles, watching, thought: Why shouldn't she be? For the vine exuded prosperity in those days, and even though those who came to see it were awed, they were also solicitous, saying: More fertilizer. Or: More food. Or: We can't let anything happen to the vine.

So by the time Charles reached manhood, any girl in the valley would have been proud to marry into the family that cared for the vine. Several vied for his attentions, but he had always loved Maida Freemont, whose father ran the pleasure palace on the hill.

Standing in the sunset, they watched the last light glint on the conservatory roof below. Charles said, "Come down in the valley and live with me."

"I don't know." Maida looked over his shoulder at the brilliant glass roof. "That place gives me the creeps."

"Nonsense," said her father, who had no business listening. "Somebody's got to take care of the vine."

"Yes," said Charles, chilled by a sudden flicker, or premonition. "I love you, Maida. I'll take care of you." He clung to her, thinking that if he could just marry her, everything might be all right. "Maida . . ."

"Yes."

He took her on a wedding trip to the ocean, a few days of freedom before they went into the conservatory to live. They came back tanned and healthy, and Charles led her through the throngs who lined the walks, waiting to see the vine.

A little self-consciously, he lifted her and carried her through the stile. "And so," he said, setting her down on the balcony inside, "here we are."

She buried her head in his neck. "Yes. Here we are."

Once they had embraced he was uneasy. He noticed a subtle change in the color of the light in the conservatory, a faint difference in the air. The air was heavier now, touched with a hint of ferment. Troubled, he took Maida's hand, hurrying her inside the house.

The rest of the family were sitting around the parlor:

Dad, Mom, Sally and Sue. They had changed from their coveralls. Mom and the girls had on lavender dresses; Dad was wearing his wine-colored shirt. They crowded around the newlyweds, and it was a minute or two before Charles realized that something was amiss.

"Where's Granddad?"

His mother said evasively, "Gone."

"Where?"

Dad shook his head. "Something took him and he died."

Sue said quietly, "It was time."

The mother rushed to make it easier. "I've turned his room into a lovely parlor for you; so you'll have a real apartment of your own."

Outside there was a sound as if the whole vine were stirring. Maida shrank against Charles and he hugged her. "Fine, Mother. That's just wonderful."

Maida was murmuring, "Oh Charlie, Charlie, take me out of here."

He wavered.

The family watched with violent eyes. They were waiting.

Nodding, he tugged at Maida. "Come on, dear." On the landing he whispered, "Trust me. Trust the vine."

And so they went upstairs. There was a sound outside, like a gigantic sigh.

Charles rose early, but the family was already at work. Sally was at the turnstile collecting money. Sue crouched on one of the wooden walks, pulling abstractedly at a weed. His mother was on a ladder at the far end of the conservatory, tying up a tendril of the vine. Charles approached her.

"Mother, something's different."

But she only frowned over her knot and wouldn't talk to him.

When they got back to the house at noon, Maida had pulled herself together. She was in the kitchen with her hair tied back and she was whistling. She said, "I've made a pie."

They finished lunch happily. Sally was full of talk about a boy she had seen. He had come through the turnstile twice, never going to the rail to gawk. He had paid just to talk to her. The mother was smiling, giving Maida a whole series of useless household hints. The father was a bit pale, abstracted.

"The pie," Maida said, cutting into it.

They were aghast. "Grape!"

Once they had finished talking to her, Charles led her to their room, trying to soothe her. "Please stop crying, darling. You just didn't understand."

"All I wanted to do was . . ."

"I know, but you hurt the vine. None of us can ever, ever hurt the vine."

Baskin stayed out in the conservatory an extra hour that evening, perhaps thinking to make amends for the grapes his bride had cut. He went along the outer walks, weeding and hoeing, and in the strange, hushed moment just before sunset he came upon his father. He lay on the ground near the outermost wall, pressed close to the earth in some uncanny communion. When Charles called, he did not stir.

Pulling and hauling, Charles got him back on the walk. "Father, you're not supposed to get on the dirt like that."

The older man looked at him, drained. "I—had to."

"Why, Father? Why?"

"You wouldn't understand."

"Father, are you all right?"

The old man shrugged him off. "Come, it's time to water the vine."

The last visitors had gone, and so they opened the cock that fed the sprinklers. They ate dinner to the sound of soft water falling. That night Charles and Maida lay close, lulled by the constant artificial rain.

The father was never quite the same; within two months he was dead, carried off by a mystery which wasted him before their eyes. As he faded, the vine prospered, growing heavy with fruit, spreading and expanding until Charles feared the conservatory would not be big enough to hold it. He worked long hours, trimming and pruning, trying to keep it within bounds, and the more he worked the less strength he seemed to have. His mother and the girls seemed to be affected too, dragging themselves about with an effort, diminishing before his eyes.

Only Maida seemed well, busy with a life which had nothing to do with the conservatory or the vine. She was pregnant, and in their dreaming talks about the future, neither Charles nor Maida mentioned the vine.

Only Sally seemed to resent the coming baby, badgering Maida because she did not help as the others did, although Sally herself spent less and less of her own time working. Instead she hung over the turnstile, talking to a boy.

"You'd better tell him to stop coming here," Charles said one night.

"Why should I? I've got to live my own life."

He frowned at Sally. "Your life is the vine."

The next day she was gone. She had taken her clothes in a cardboard suitcase, running away with the boy. They had one postcard from a distant city. GET OUT BEFORE IT'S TOO LATE. There was no return address.

Sue shook her head over it. "We'll have to work harder to make up for her."

"It won't help," the mother said from her corner. Her voice sagged with despair. "Nothing will help."

"Don't say that," Charles said sharply. "We have to take care of the vine."

Deep in pregnancy, Maida snapped, "Damn the vine."

Since Charles couldn't find his mother to help him when his son was born, he and Sue had to midwife.

When it was all over, Charles went out on the walks and called for the old lady, full of the news. He found her at last, pressed against the earth as his father had been, and he had to pull to get her free. He imagined something snapped as he pulled her away from the soil. Frightened, he took her back to the house and put her to bed. Even when she was stronger, he would not let her leave the house. He and Sue carried on alone, because they had to. The mother died anyway. They buried her in the family plot, where she could feed the vine.

There were four of them in the house now: Charles and Maida and the baby—and Sue, who wasted before their eyes. Charles might have despaired, he might have fled if it hadn't been for the baby. The baby was his future and his hope: it would grow strong and prosper, carrying on the Baskin tradition of caring for the vine.

"We'll have a girl soon," he said to Maida, beaming.

On the other side of the fire, Sue put her hands to her lips; her fingers fluttered across her face. Before they could stop her, she was on her feet and running. When he went out on the porch, Charles could hear her footsteps, desperate and fast. But it was dark and the great vine creaked above him. With a shudder, he went back inside.

They never saw Sue again, and so Maida had to pen the baby in the cottage and go out and help him with the vine. She was quick and capable, and now that she had borne a child here, she seemed strangely reconciled to life inside the conservatory, at one with the others who had labored here. She and Charles worked well, but he began to notice changes in her. He would find her on the farthest catwalk, her cheek pressed against the glass outer wall. It was around this time that Charles found Sue's skeleton, suspended in a cocoon of green. He freed it and buried it quickly, so Maida would not have to see. The earth was alive with twisting tendrils, and he jumped back in alarm.

"We'll go," he said, biting through his lower lip.

"I'll take her and the baby and get out of here."

But it was too late. She did not answer his urgent cries, and he found her at last, lying pressed to the earth just outside the cottage door. When he pulled her up she smiled, blind but still loving. Where it had touched the earth, her skin was flecked with tiny broken veins. He took her in his arms and ran with her, collapsing outside by the road. When the police took them to the hospital, Charles called Maida's father.

"Mr. Freemont, Maida and I are leaving as soon as she's well enough to travel."

"You'll be all right," Freemont said, not listening. "I'll look after Maida here. You'd better get back and do for that vine."

"You don't understand, we have to get *away* from it . . ."

The old man turned him towards the conservatory. "She'll be all right, son. You just get back to work."

Because there was nothing else to do he went, but his mind was seething with plans. When Maida got better, he would take her and the baby; he would steal a car if he had to, and they would drive and drive until they were safe.

"She's dead," the father said, weeping at the turnstile.

"The vine killed her," Baskin said wildly.

The old man patted him. "There, there. It's coming on harvest time. You know how the visitors love that . . ."

"But I have to . . ."

"You have to carry on for Maida. For the valley. We all depend on you."

Before he could protest, the old man pushed a rake into his hand. A crew began installing an automatic turnstile.

"Tell you what," Freemont said. "We'll put up a 'No Visitors' sign. Give you time to mourn."

"But there isn't . . ." Baskin went on, to the empty

conservatory ". . . time to mourn. There's only time to take care of the vine."

Its demands took all his waking hours. He would pen the baby on the porch where he could watch it, and if he left the baby unattended that last night, it was hardly his fault. He heard a snap and a groan in the distance, and ran to investigate. The vine had broken a pane of glass. He was about to turn back to the house and the baby when a leafy coil dropped around his arm, holding him as if to say: Listen.

Impatient, he wrenched himself free. In growing panic, he began to run.

He couldn't have made it: no one could have made it in time. The baby had climbed or had been lifted out of the pen, and it was playing in the dirt in front of the house. Baskin shouted, splitting his throat, but before the baby could hear or try to respond, a root whipped out of the ground, looped itself around the child's neck and pulled it into the earth.

He imagined he heard a cosmic belch.

Flinging himself on the dirt, he tore at it in a fury, but there was no sign of the child, not his cap or his rattle, not even a bone. In his pain and rage Baskin dug deep, hacking at roots and gouging the earth. The soil was alive, fighting him, and he barely tore himself free.

He retreated to the porch, breathing hard. Going into the house, he collected papers and sticks and rags, and he followed the walks to the great trunk, making a pyre about its base. He soaked the whole in kerosene and set fire to it.

So it was that Charles Baskin waged war on the vine.

Dancing back to avoid the heat, he cursed it, thinking it would all be over soon, but as he watched the sprinkler system let loose, perhaps triggered by a tentacle of the vine. When the smoke cleared, he saw that the vine was scarcely damaged, with the fire out, it was drenching itself from within, bathing the wounded trunk in sap.

Next Baskin attacked it with a chain saw, but before he had gone far the vine was dropping tendrils from every frame and division of the arbor, and every tendril had begun to root. Fresh tendrils took the saw and tried to turn it on him; he had to hack his way to safety, fleeing the conservatory in a growing despair. He thought to tip a vat of lye on the ground, but before he could get close enough, roots were coming through the earth outside the glass house, twining around the vat and reaching for Baskin himself. He would have attacked the trunk again, but the conservatory was already impenetrable. The thing had surrounded itself with a thick armature of loops and fibrous whips, and he could never get close enough to harm it; it would get him first.

Desperate, he hit on a final plan: if he could not damage the plant, then he would smash the conservatory, and the first frost would kill the vine.

He had broken only three panes when the angry plant whipped out and snared him. He was fighting feebly when the first truck came over the horizon. They were coming out from town to investigate.

"Thank God," he said to his first rescuer. "Oh thank God."

The man peered at him through the greenery. "What happened?"

"We've got to kill it," Baskin said, thinking: Now they'll see. They have to see. "We have to get it before it gets us."

"He was trying to hurt it," the man said to someone behind him. "Looks like we were just in time."

Baskin gasped, still not understanding. "Just in time."

They stood back and let the vine finish what it was doing. Then they held a lottery, selecting the new keeper on the spot. The lucky winner sent a friend back to town to tell his wife, and then he went forward, opening the

double doors to the conservatory. As he approached, the vine withdrew its tendrils, rewinding them neatly on the arbor. Only slightly uneasy, the new keeper whispered, into the dimness:
"Are you all right?"

Winston

Edna Waziki was beside herself by the time theirs came. She talked about nothing else for months after they put in the order and she sat by the window for hours, and when the truck finally pulled in to the drive she screamed a scream that brought the entire family on the run. The delivery man came to the door with a little travelling case, with a handle on top and holes poked in the end, and Edna giggled and the kids laughed and danced and jumped around while Edna's husband Artie paid the driver and they jiggled uncontrollably while Artic fumbled with the catch.

"It says here his name is Winston," Edna said, turning the card so Margie and Little Art could read the name. "Now step back, we don't want to scare him all at once."

Artie scowled into the suitcase. "Well where is the little bastard?"

"Artie, *please*." Edna bent down, calling softly.

"Tchum on, Winston, tchum on."

Margie said, "Daddy, Daddy, I can see him."

Little Art was poking a stick into the opening. "Daddy, Daddy, here he comes!"

"Damn foolishness," Artie said, but he crowded around with his wife and children and they watched Winston come blinking into the light.

Margie gasped. "Oh Daddy, he's *teeny*."

"In he cute, oh, Artie, in he cute."

Artie snorted. "He sure don't look like much."

"You can't tell when they're little like this," Edna said. "But you just wait till he grows up!"

Margie was snickering. "Oh look, he made a puddle."

"Of course he has, he's nervous." Edna swept Winston to her bosom. "Poor thing, you poor little thing."

"Runt like that," Artie said, "he's never gonna come to anything."

"Honey, didn't you see his pedigree?"

"Oh Mama, he looks like a monkey."

"Shh, you'll hurt his feelings."

"Here Winston, here Winston." Little Art tried to make Winston take the stick.

"You leave him alone." Edna held Winston protectively; Winston was crying.

"He won't even take the stick."

"He'll take it," Artie said ominously. "He better take it. Lord knows I *paid* enough."

Edna hugged Winston protectively. "He's upset. He'll feel better when I clean him up."

Artie accused her: "You said he was guaranteed."

"He *is* guaranteed," Edna sid, taking Winston to the bedroom; in the doorway she turned and said defensively, "You'll just have to wait, it all takes time."

She spent about an hour on him and when she came out he was calmer, much quieter, and he had stopped crying; he even sat up at the table with them, brought to adult height by a stack of city telephone books. He was about four, small-boned and blond, with a little blue romper suit buttoned fore and aft and large brown eyes which crackled with intelligence. He looked at them all in turn but he wouldn't touch his dish.

"See that," Artie said in exasperation. "Five thousand dollars and he won't even touch his dish."

"He'll eat," Edna said. "He just doesn't know us yet."

"Well he *better* get to know us. Five thousand dollars down the drain."

"It's *not* down the drain," Edna said; she was getting too upset to talk. "He'll make us proud, you just wait."

Freddy Kramer came in just then, to pick Artie up for bowling. "So this is it," he said, giving Winston the once-over.

"First family on the block to have one," Artie said, with dawning pride. "I guess you might call it a kind of a status symbol."

"Don't look like much."

"You ought to see his pedigree." Looking at Freddy, who would never be able to afford one, Artie allowed himself to be expansive. "Lady writer and a college professor. Eye Q. a hundred and sixty, guaranteed."

Edna stroked Winston's fine blond hair. "Winston's going to college." It pleased her to see that Artie was smiling.

"Kid's gonna get his Ph.D."

Edna took Artie's hand under the table, saying in a low voice, "Oh Artie, you *are* glad. I knew you would be."

Freddy Kramer was looking at Winston with a look bordering on naked jealousy. "What gave you the idea?"

"Edna seen the ad." Artie went all squashy; Edna was massaging his knee. "And anything my baby wants . . ."

"You won't be sorry, Artie. Winston's gonna major

in physics. He might even invent the next atomic bomb."

Freddy's lips were moving; he seemed to be figuring under his breath. "How big of a down payment would they want?"

"Depends on the product," Edna said.

"Now this one," Artie said, slapping Winston's shoulder, "this one's gonna support us in our old age. Ph.D. and one-letter man guaranteed. He might get our name in the papers, according to the ad."

Edna said vaguely, "There's something about a Guggenheim."

Winston started crying.

"Why Winston, what's the matter?"

"Little Art kicked him," Margie said.

"Well you kids keep off him until you learn to play with him nice."

"You can't get 'em like this no more," Artie was saying to Freddy Kramer. "Parents had ten and retired to Europe on the take."

Freddy rubbed his nose. "Maybe if Flo and I sold the car..."

Artie proffered a piece of bread to Winston; Winston looked at it distastefully but he took it. "See, he likes me. Hey honey, he likes me."

"Of course he does," Edna said with pride. "He's our son."

Winston gave her a sudden sharp look which embarrassed her for no reason. Then he finished the bread and cleared his throat.

Artie was saying to Freddy, "... and if you can't get them into Exeter they're guaranteed for Culver at least."

"Shhh, honey, he's going to say something."

"... It ain't every steamfitter that has a kid in Culver, ya know."

"Shh."

Winston spoke, "Wiwyiam F. Buckwey is a weactionawy."

"Hey Freddy, did ya hear that?"

"I really gotta hand it to you," Freddy said.

They didn't go bowling that night after all; they all sat around the living room and first they had Winston read the daily papers to them, even the editorials, and when he was done they listened to him analyze the political situation and then Edna brought them all cake and they had Winston predict the season's batting averages while Artie wrote them down and then Winston wrote a poem about autumn and then Winston began to suck his thumb; Edna sent the other kids to bed and they went, complaining because Winston got to stay up and they knew he was going to end up with the rest of the cake; the grownups listened to Winston some more and then Winston and Artie got into a kind of political argument, Artie must have hurt his feelings a little, calling him a squirt and too young to know anything about *anything*, because Winston began to sniffle, and Edna said they were going to have to let her put him to bed now, he just looked tired to death.

She took him up to the front room, where they had laid in the complete works of Bulwer-Lytton and the eleventh edition of the Britannica; she showed Winston the globe and the autoclave and the slide rule and the drafting board, thinking he would give little cries of delight and perhaps sit down at the desk at once and compose something on the silent keyboard they had bought him, but instead he clung to her shoulder and wouldn't even look. Finally she said, "Why honey, what's the matter?"

"I want my diddy," Winston said.

She found it finally, a tattered square of blanket jammed in the back of the travelling case, and once she had restored it to him Winston let her give him a bath and put him in his pajamas with the bunny feet; even in his pajamas he had that pedigreed look: his ankles and wrists were small and his fingers were long and she found herself wishing he looked just a *little* cuddlier, just a little more like one of *her* babies, but she suppressed the thought quickly.

In bed, she said to Artie, "Just imagine. Right here, our own little Ph.D." She hugged him. "Isn't it wonderful?"

"I don't know." Artie was looking at the ceiling. "I think he's kind of fresh."

The Wazikis were awakened by a hubbub in the back yard. Artie found Little Art and some of Little Art's friends grappling in the early-morning dirt and when he pried them off he found Winston, white and shaken and biting his lip so the other kids wouldn't see him cry. He extricated Winston and set him on the back stoop and then turned to Little Art and Margie; they sniggered and wouldn't look at him.

"What's the matter, Winston?"

But Winston wouldn't say anything, he only sat there wearing what Artie would learn to call his Hamlet look.

Little Art elbowed Artie, with a dirty snicker. "You got rooked."

"I *what*?"

"Dummy here can't even catch the ball."

Winston had stopped shaking. "My father couldn't catch a ball either," he said coldly, "and he was wunner-up for the Nobel Pwize."

There was something about Winston's attitude that Artie didn't like, but he cuffed Little Art all the same and said, "We didn't pay for him to catch the ball, dummy. You keep your hands off the merchandise."

"If he's so damn smart why can't he catch the ball?"

"Shut up and come on inside."

At breakfast Margie brought out her geography homework and Artie and Winston had a little set-to about what was the capital of the Cameroons; Winston was right of course and Edna made Artie apologize and then she had to smooth it over because it was obvious to everybody that the whole thing had put Artie on edge.

"Four-year-old kid. Four-year-old *kid*."

"I'm sowwy," said Winston, who in addition to the 160 I.Q. was nobody's fool, "they used to make me study all the time."

"Well they didn't teach ya manners."

"There there," Margie said, trying to smooth the frown from Artie's brow. "Just wait till you see the terrarium."

He pushed her fingers away. "What in hell is a terrarium?"

"I don't know, but Winston and I are going to make one."

"I don't want the kid playing with no explosives, and that's that."

Winston had on his Hamlet look. "Anything you say, Mr. Waziki."

Artie decided the kid *was* trying. "You can call me Pop."

"O.K., Mr. Waziki."

At work he found that Freddy Kramer had spread the word; he was something of a celebrity in the shop. By lunch time he was basking in the glow.

"Hundred and sixty," he said in the face of their doubt and envy, "and he calls me Pop."

All the same he was more gratified than he should have been when he came home from work to find Little Art and Winston at it again. Little Art had the Britannica on his lap and he was barking at Winston:

"Who was at the Diet of Worms?"

Winston made a couple of stabs at it and subsided in embarrassment.

"Hey Pop, you been rooked."

Artie said weakly, "Lay off, kid."

"Hundred and sixty and he don't even know who was at the Diet of Worms."

Winston looked at his hands apologetically. "I'm bwand new."

"Well you just find out, kid. It's your business to know."

Edna swept Winston to her bosom, noting uncomfortably that he was all knees and elbows. "You just lay off him."

Winston dug his chin in her shoulder. "I want my diddy," Winston said.

Even Edna had to admit Winston was too intelligent to hang onto a silly piece of blanket, it didn't look good, and so she had Winston help her wrap up his diddy and put it away, and then they sent him up to his room to learn all he could about Weimeraner dogs and when he came out Artie got into a rage because he hadn't learned a thing about Weimeraners even though he had the whole V volume of the Britannica to look it up in because never mind what the wise kid kept trying to tell them, Artie knew it was spelled just like it sounds.

And as if he hadn't learned his lesson Winston had the nerve to dispute Artie over a point of steamfitting, the thing Artie knew best, and when they looked it up it turned out Winston was right. Then Little Artie wanted Winston to leg-wrestle, and expensive as Winston was, Artie let him because he, Artie, was the head of the family and if Winston was going to live with the Wazikis he was going to have to shape up.

The next day Edna had her bridge group and she dressed Winston in his pale tan romper suit, the one with the bunny-rabbit on the pocket, and she propped him up with his pocket Spinoza and the ladies all made a terrific fuss over him, chucking his chin and feeding him fudge and making him recite until finally he got nervous or something and he threw up right on the cretonne slipcover, Edna's favorite. She cleaned up the mess and brought him back in his *blue* romper suit but he wasn't so much of a hit after that.

"Isn't he kind of *sensitive*?" Maud Wilson said.

"He's bred for brains," Edna said patiently. "When they're bred for brains you've got to put up with a lot."

Melinda Patterson smiled a saccharine smile. "I just don't know whether it's worth it in the long run, putting up with all the mess."

"Winston is going to get his Ph.D." Edna saw she was losing them, and she went on quickly. "And next week he's going to win the Bonanza contest, just you wait and see."

She was sorry the minute she said it; the Bonanza contest was a kind of crossword puzzle and she didn't know whether Winston was trained for that kind of thing, but she had laid Winston on the line and he was just going to have to follow through; maybe he would win and the prize money would make up for all the trouble he had given them. If Winston won they would all get their pictures in the papers together, and it would be a lot easier to be *friends* with Winston after that. They might even let him have his diddy back. As soon as the ladies left she told Winston about the contest and when he cried she tried to cuddle him, but he wouldn't kiss her and she had to spank him. Then she got eight dictionaries, a thesaurus and that week's Bonanza puzzle and sent him to his room.

He tried, he tried for days, and when they came to check on him at the end of the week he said: "It's hopeless."

Artie glowered. "Don't you tell me what's hopeless."

"Look." He made them read one of last week's answers. THERE'S NO PLACE LIKE . . . and a four-letter word. "The answer is ROME because while there are many HOMES there is only one ROME." He said, "See? It's a hoked-up awbitwawy cheat."

"Do the puzzle, Winston."

"But it's all chance."

Artie shook him. "Don't you tell me what's chance."

Evelyn Cartwright was the first on the phone when Winston didn't win. "I just thought maybe he hadn't *entered*," she said in honeyed tones. Edna was grim. "He entered five hundred and seventy-eight times."

"I.Q. one-sixty," Evelyn Cartwright said with a musical snigger. "All that money down the drain."

The guys in the shop laughed so hard that Artie came home early. "Kid just don't know his place. I'm gonna make him learn his place."

Edna thought maybe if she cut down on Winston's rations it would sharpen his brains, so she put him on bread and water and a little fish: brain food, according to the books. Could she help it if some part of her insisted that she serve rich stews to Artie and the kids at the same time? Could she help it if determination hardened her heart so that she didn't even watch Winston's tiny, tortured face as the others devoured ice cream and sugar cookies, and fell on meatloaves like twenty-one-inch shells and devoured coconut custard pies?

Artie decided a little outdoor work would put Winston in trim and build his character too so he turned him over to Margic and Little Art for a couple of hours every afternoon; they tried to make him catch the ball and they made him run foot races and practice broad-jumping and Artie always let it go on a little longer than it should have because after all, the kid had to turn out a one-letter man, it was in the guarantee.

What killed them was, after all they'd paid for him he snivelled all the time, even after Edna let him hang up the snapshot of his father the professor and his mother the lady writer sunning at Biarritz; they had sent it in a letter reminding the Wazikis that the true parents were entitled to half of Winston's future earnings, and it burned Artie so much that he tore it up and jumped up and down on the pieces and wouldn't let Winston see it at all, not even the part where they sent their love. All that money, and Winston could hardly keep his mind on the dumbest questions; Edna's next bridge gathering was a real washout, Winston cried the whole time, and all the ladies could talk about was how peaky he looked.

Artie thought maybe a Sane Mind in a Sound Body and from then on Winston slept on the screen porch for his health, they even let him have a blanket because it was kind of cold.

Artie's birthday was coming up and he had taken so much guff from Freddy Kramer and the guys from the shop that he knew he had to show them, he would have a big beer party on his birthday, by that time Winston would be shaped up from the brain food and all that sleeping on the porch. He would have a big beer party on his birthday, he would get everybody greased and then he would have Winston come in and do his stuff. As it turned out they probably did drink too much, and maybe Artie did forget about Winston being outside for his constitutional, and maybe it was snowing by the time somebody remembered and they brought him in; maybe that's why all he did was stand there in his romper suit with his knees knocking and his jaw set in his Hamlet look.

Or maybe it was just plain stubbornness; whatever it was, Artie gave him a cuff and said, "Okay, Winston, tell the guys about the Diet of Worms."

"Yes, Mr. Waziki."

Artie gave him a belt. "And call me Pop."

"Yes, Mr. Waziki."

Artie gave him another belt and he started off on the Diet of Worms but he only got out a couple of lines before his mind wandered or something and he began staring at some spot in a corner and when Artie prodded him he turned to Artie with his face flaming and a look that bordered on apology and said, "I'm sowwy. I f-forget."

"What, forget." Artie poked him harder because all the guys were laughing. "What forget?"

Winston was shaking pretty hard, his knees were knocking; nerves, probably, Artie decided; Winston said, "I j-just."

"Awright, awright," Artie said, because the guys were pushing him and Winston had better hurry up and do *something*. He tried to steer him into familiar territory: "Tell the gang about the Weimeraner dog."

"Hell," Freddy Kramer said, egging the other guys on. "I bet he can't even add."

"Yeah," said somebody. "Big deal, Artie. What else did ya bring?"

Artie gripped Winston by the shoulders; the other guys were getting ugly and he had to do something quick. He shook Winston, hard, hissing, "Times tables. Give 'em the times tables."

Winston just rolled up his eyes with an agonized, forgive-me look. His teeth were chattering so hard now that he couldn't even talk. Still he made a brave beginning: "W-wun."

"See," Artie said quickly, "he's about to give you the one-times."

"The hell he is, look at him."

Winston's face was flaming now, his eyes feverish, and when Artie pressed him he couldn't even talk. The guys were getting ugly and if Winston didn't do something in a minute they were all going to walk out on his birthday party and Artie would be finished down at the shop.

"He's going to give you the *times table*," Artie said doggedly, and he kept on shaking Winston.

"Forget it, Artie."

"Forget it *hell*." They were all milling and fuming and he had to act fast so he picked Winston up by the sailor collar. "Back in a minute. I'm gonna teach him, I'm gonna teach him for once and for all."

Then he took Winston upstairs and he got Edna's silver hairbrush and turned him over his knee, muttering, "Gonna teach him a *lesson*," and when he finally stopped spanking Winston he set him back on his feet. Winston's legs buckled and his eyes rolled back so all Artie could see was the whites. He kept on for a couple of minutes, trying to make Winston stand up or answer or *something* and after a while he got scared and went down and called Edna, noting only in passing that the guys must have got depressed, hearing Winston yelling and all, everybody was gone.

"I guess I hurt him," he said as Edna rushed past him.

"You ruined him, you went and ruined him." Edna was crying over Winston's crumpled body.

"Five thousand dollars shot," Artie said.

Winston began to moan so they called the company doctor, after all, it was in the guarantee. Winston turned out to be in a coma or something, he was burning up with fever and they sat up with wet compresses and stuff for several days and when Winston began to come out of it they noticed something funny and they called the doctor in again. After he had been with Winston for several minutes he came out and Edna gripped him by the elbow saying: "All right? Is he going to be all right?"

The doctor looked weary beyond description. "With a lot of care he'll be all right."

Shrewdly, Artie followed up. "One-sixty and all?"

"He'll be all right, but he'll never think again."

"Then we get our money back."

"Read your contract," the doctor said, as if he had been through all this before. "You'll find your baby intellectuals are only guaranteed against failure."

"Failure, let me tell you about failure..."

But the doctor was moving towards the door. "Not against personal damage or acts of God."

Artie had the doctor by the shoulders now and they were in the doorway, wrangling, but Edna paid no attention; instead she took a bowl of chicken soup and crept up to Winston's room.

He was pale and diminished, lying there under the covers, but he looked more or less all right. He recognized her when she came in and he began to moan.

She stroked his forehead. "All right, baby, you're going to be all right."

"Sick." Winston was blubbering. "Sick."

"Mommy make you all right." Because he wouldn't stop crying she thought fast. "Diddy? Winston want his diddy?"

"Diddy," Winston said, and when she produced it, took it to his bosom with a look of bliss.

"That's a boy."

Winston stopped stroking his cheek with his diddy and looked around the room until his eyes rested on the globe, He tried to sit up. "Baw?"

"Ball, Winston. Ball."

"Baw."

"That's my baby. Ball. That's my baby, baby boy."

"Baw? Baw?"

"Him's a *sweet* boy." When he smiled like that he looked just like Margie or Little Artie. She swept him to her bosom. "Him can be my baby boy."

"Ba-by?"

She had an apple pie cooking; she would give the whole thing to him. "Baby, poor baby." She smoothed his hair back from his forehead. "All dat finking wadn't *dood* for him."

The Food Farm

So here I am, warden-in-charge, fattening them up for our leader, Tommy Fango; here I am laying on the banana pudding and the milkshakes and the cream-and-brandy cocktails, going about like a technician, gauging their effect on haunch and thigh when all the time it is I who love him, I who could have pleased him eternally if only life had broken differently. But I am scrawny now, I am swept like a leaf around corners, battered by the slightest wind. My elbows rattle against my ribs and I have to spend half the day in bed so a gram or two of what I eat will stay with me, for if I do not, the fats and creams will vanish, burned up in my own insatiable furnace, and what little flesh I have will melt away.

Cruel as it may sound, I know where to place the blame.

It was vanity, all vanity, and I hate them most for that. It was not my vanity, for I have always been a simple soul; I reconciled myself early to reenforced chairs and loose garments, to the spattering of remarks. Instead of heeding them I plugged in, and I would have been happy to let it go at that, going through life with my radio in my bodice, for while I never drew cries of admiration, no one ever blanched and turned away.

But they were vain and in their vanity my frail father, my pale, scrawny mother saw me not as an entity but a reflection on themselves. I flush with shame to remember the excuses they made for me. "She takes after May's side of the family," my father would say, denying any responsibility. "It's only baby fat," my mother would say, jabbing her elbow into my soft flank. "Nelly is big for her age." Then she would jerk furiously, pulling my voluminous smock down to cover my knees. That was when they still consented to be seen with me. In that period they would stuff me with pies and roasts before we went anywhere, filling me up so I would not gorge myself in public. Even so I had to take thirds, fourths, fifths and so I was a humiliation to them.

In time I was too much for them and they stopped taking me out; they made no more attempts to explain. Instead they tried to think of ways to make me look better; the doctors tried the fool's poor battery of pills; they tried to make me join a club. For a while my mother and I did exercises; we would sit on the floor, she in a black leotard, I in my smock. Then she would do the brisk one-two, one-two and I would make a few passes at my toes. But I had to listen, I had to plug in, and after I was plugged in naturally I had to find something to eat; Tommy might sing and I always ate when Tommy sang, and so I would leave her there on the floor, still going one-two, one-two. For a while after that they tried locking up the food. Then they began to cut into my meals.

That was the cruelest time. They would refuse me bread, they would plead and cry, plying me with lettuce and telling me it was all for my own good. My own good. Couldn't they hear my vitals crying out? I fought, I screamed, and when that failed I suffered in silent obedience until finally hunger drove me into the streets. I would lie in bed, made brave by the Monets and Barry Arkin and the Philadons coming in over the radio, and Tommy (there was never enough; I heard him a hundred times a day and it was never enough; how bitter that seems now!). I would hear them and then when my parents were asleep I would unplug and go out into the neighborhood. The first few nights I begged, throwing myself on the mercy of passers-by and then plunging into the bakery, bringing home everything I didn't eat right there in the shop. I got money quickly enough; I didn't even have to ask. Perhaps it was my bulk, perhaps it was my desperate subverbal cry of hunger; I found I had only to approach and the money was mine. As soon as they saw me, people would whirl and bolt, hurling a purse or wallet into my path as if to slow me in my pursuit; they would be gone before I could even express my thanks. Once I was shot at. Once a stone lodged itself in my flesh.

At home my parents continued with their tears and pleas. They persisted with their skim milk and their chops, ignorant of the life I lived by night. In the daytime I was complaisant, dozing between snacks, feeding on the sounds which played in my ear, coming from the radio concealed in my dress. Then, when night fell, I unplugged; it gave a certain edge to things, knowing I would not plug in again until I was ready to eat. Some nights this only meant going to one of the caches in my room, bringing forth bottles and cartons and cans. On other nights I had to go into the streets, finding money where I could. Then I would lay in a new supply of cakes and rolls and baloney from the delicatessen and several cans of ready-made frosting and perhaps a fletch of bacon or some ham; I would toss in a basket of oranges to ward off scurvy and a carton of candy bars for quick energy. Once I had enough I would go back to my room, concealing food here and there, rearranging my nest of pillows and comforters. I would open the first pie or the first half-gallon of ice cream and then, as I began, I would plug in.

You had to plug in; everybody that mattered was plugged in. It was our bond, our solace and our power, and it wasn't a matter of being distracted, or occupying time. The sound was what mattered, that and the fact that fat or thin, asleep or awake, you were important when you plugged in, and you knew that through fire and flood and adversity, through contumely and hard times there was this single bond, this common heritage; strong or weak, eternally gifted or wretched and ill-loved, we were all plugged in.

Tommy, beautiful Tommy Fango, the others paled to nothing next to him. Everybody heard him in those days; they played him two or three times an hour but you never knew when it would be so you were plugged in and listening hard every living moment; you ate, you slept, you drew breath for the moment when they would put on one of Tommy's records, you waited for his voice to fill the room. Cold cuts and cupcakes and game hens came and went during that period in my life, but one thing was constant; I always had a cream pie thawing and when they played the first bars of "When a Widow" and Tommy's voice first flexed and uncurled, I was ready, I would eat the cream pie during Tommy's midnight show. The whole world waited in those days; we waited through endless sunlight, through nights of drumbeats and monotony, we all waited for Tommy Fango's records, and we waited for that whole unbroken hour of Tommy, his midnight show. He came on live at midnight in those days; he sang, broadcasting from the Hotel Riverside, and that was beautiful, but more important, he talked, and while he was talking he made everything all right. Nobody was lonely when Tommy talked; he brought us all together on that midnight show, he talked and made us powerful, he talked and finally he sang. You have to imagine what it was like, me in the night, Tommy, the pie. In a while I would go to a place where I had to live on Tommy and only Tommy, to a time when hearing Tommy would bring back the pie, all the poor lost pies. . . .

Tommy's records, his show, the pie . . . that was perhaps the happiest period of my life. I would sit and listen and I would eat and eat and eat. So great was my bliss that it became torture to put away the food at daybreak; it grew harder and harder for me to hide the cartons and the cans and the bottles, all the residue of my happiness. Perhaps a bit of bacon fell into the register; perhaps an egg rolled under the bed and began to smell. All right, perhaps I did become careless, continuing my revels into the morning, or I may have been thoughtless enough to leave a jelly roll unfinished on the rug. I became aware that they were watching, lurking just outside my door, plotting as I ate. In time they broke in on me, weeping and pleading, lamenting over every ice cream carton and crumb of pie; then they threatened. Finally they restored the food they had taken from me in the daytime, thinking to curtail my eating at night. Folly. By that time I needed it all, I shut myself in with it and would not listen. I ignored their cries of hurt pride, their outpourings of wounded vanity, their puny little threats. Even if I had listened, I could not have forestalled what happened next.

I was so happy that last day. There was a Smithfield ham, mine, and I remember a jar of cherry preserves, mine, and I remember bacon, pale and white on Italian bread. I remember sounds downstairs and before I could take warning, an assault, a company of uniformed attendants, the sting of a hypodermic gun. Then the ten of them closed in and grappled me into a sling, or net, and heaving and straining, they bore me down the stairs. I'll never forgive you, I cried, as they bundled me into the ambulance. I'll never forgive you, I bellowed as my mother in a last betrayal took away my radio, and I cried out one last time, as my father removed a hambone from my breast: I'll never forgive you, And I never have.

It is painful to describe what happened next. I remember three days of horror and agony, of being too weak, finally, to cry out or claw the walls. Then at last I was quiet and they moved me into a sunny, pastel, chintz-bedizened room. I remember that there were flowers on the dresser and someone watching me.

"What are you in for?" she said.

I could barely speak for weakness. "Despair."

"Hell with that," she said, chewing. "You're in for food."

"What are you eating?" I tried to raise my head.

"Chewing. Inside of the mouth. It helps."

"I'm going to die."

"Everybody thinks that at first. I did." She tilted her head in an attitude of grace. "You know, this is a very exclusive school."

Her name was Ramona and as I wept silently, she filled me in. This was a last resort for the few who could afford to send their children here. They prettied it up with a schedule of therapy, exercise, massage; we would wear dainty pink smocks and talk of art and theater; from time to time we would attend classes in elocution and hygiene. Our parents would say with pride that we were away at Faircrest, an elegant finishing school; we knew better—it was a prison and we were being starved.

"It's a world I never made," said Ramona, and I knew that her parents were to blame, even as mine were. Her mother liked to take the children into hotels and casinos, wearing her thin daughters like a garland of jewels. Her father followed the sun on his private yacht, with the pennants flying and his children on the fantail, lithe and tanned. He would pat his flat, tanned belly and look at Ramona in disgust. When it was no longer possible to hide her, he gave in to blind pride. One night they came in a launch and took her away. She had been here six months now, and had lost almost a hundred pounds. She must have been monumental in her prime; she was still huge.

"We live from day to day," she said. "But you don't know the worst."

"My radio," I said in a spasm of fear. "They took away my radio."

"There is a reason," she said. "They call it therapy."

I was mumbling in my throat, in a minute I would scream.

"Wait." With ceremony, she pushed aside a picture and touched a tiny switch and then, like sweet balm for my panic, Tommy's voice flowed into the room.

When I was quiet she said, "You only hear him once a day."

"No."

"But you can hear him any time you want to. You hear him when you need him most."

But we were missing the first few bars and so we shut up and listened, and after "When a Widow" was over we sat quietly for a moment, her resigned, me weeping, and then Ramona threw another switch and the Sound filtered into the room, and it was almost like being plugged in.

"Try not to think about it."

"I'll die."

"If you think about it you *will* die. You have to learn to use it instead. In a minute they will come with lunch," Ramona said and as The Screamers sang sweet background, she went on in a monotone: "A chop. One lousy chop with a piece of lettuce and maybe some gluten bread. I pretend it's a leg of lamb, that works if you eat very, very slowly and think about Tommy the whole time; then if you look at your picture of Tommy you can turn the lettuce into anything you want, Caesar salad or a whole smorgasbord, and if you say his name over and over you can pretend a whole bombe or torte if you want to and..."

"I'm going to pretend a ham and kidney pie and a watermelon filled with chopped fruits and Tommy and I are in the Rainbow Room and we're going to finish up with Fudge Royale..." I almost drowned in my own saliva; in the background I could almost hear Tommy and I could hear Ramona saying, "Capon, Tommy would like capon, canard à l'orange, Napoleons, tomorrow we will save Tommy for lunch and listen while we eat..." and I thought about that, I thought about listening and imagining whole cream pies and I went on, "... lemon pie, rice pudding, a whole Edam cheese... I think I'm going to live."

The matron came in the next morning at breakfast, and stood as she would every day, tapping red fingernails on one svelte hip, looking on in revulsion as we fell on the glass of orange juice and the hard-boiled egg. I was too weak to control myself; I heard a shrill sniveling sound and realized only from her expression that it was my own voice: "Please, just some bread, a stick of butter, anything, I could lick the dishes if you'd let me, only please don't leave me like this, please..." I can still see her sneer as she turned her back.

I felt Ramona's loyal hand on my shoulder. "There's always toothpaste but don't use too much at once or they'll come and take it away from you."

I was too weak to rise and so she brought it and we shared the tube and talked about all the banquets we had ever known, and when we got tired of that we talked about Tommy, and when that failed, Ramona went to the switch and we heard "When a Widow," and that helped for a while, and then we decided that tomorrow we would put off "When a Widow" until bedtime because then we would have something to look forward to all day. Then lunch came and we both wept.

It was not just hunger: after a while the stomach

begins to devour itself and the few grams you toss it at mealtimes assuage it so that in time the appetite itself begins to fail. After hunger comes depression. I lay there, still too weak to get about, and in my misery I realized that they could bring me roast pork and watermelon and Boston cream pie without ceasing; they could gratify all my dreams and I would only weep helplessly, because I no longer had the strength to eat. Even then, when I thought I had reached rock bottom, I had not comprehended the worst. I noticed it first in Ramona. Watching her at the mirror, I said, in fear:

"You're thinner."

She turned with tears in her eyes. "Nelly, I'm not the only one."

I looked around at my own arms and saw that she was right: there was one less fold of flesh above the elbow; there was one less wrinkle at the wrist. I turned my face to the wall and all Ramona's talk of food and Tommy did not comfort me. In desperation she turned on Tommy's voice, but as he sang I lay back and contemplated the melting of my own flesh.

"If we stole a radio we could hear him again," Ramona said, trying to soothe me. "We could hear him when he sings tonight."

Tommy came to Faircrest on a visit two days later, for reasons that I could not then understand. All the other girls lumbered into the assembly hall to see him, thousands of pounds of agitated flesh. It was that morning that I discovered I could walk again, and I was on my feet, struggling into the pink tent in a fury to get to Tommy, when the matron intercepted me.

"Not you, Nelly."

"I have to get to Tommy. I have to hear him sing."

"Next time, maybe." With a look of naked cruelty she added, "You're a disgrace. You're still too gross."

I lunged, but it was too late; she had already shot the bolt. And so I sat in the midst of my diminishing body, suffering while every other girl in the place listened to him sing. I knew then that I had to act; I would regain myself somehow, I would find food and regain my flesh and then I would go to Tommy. I would use force if I had to, but I would hear him sing. I raged through the room all that morning, hearing the shrieks of five hundred girls, the thunder of their feet, but even when I pressed myself against the wall I could not hear Tommy's voice.

Yet Ramona, when she came back to the room, said the most interesting thing. It was some time before she could speak at all, but in her generosity she played "When a Widow" while she regained herself, and then she spoke:

"He came for something, Nelly. He came for something he didn't find."

"Tell about what he was wearing. Tell what his throat did when he sang."

"He looked at all the *before* pictures, Nelly. The matron was trying to make him look at the *afters* but he kept looking at the *befores* and shaking his head and then he found one and put it in his pocket and if he hadn't found it, he wasn't going to sing."

I could feel my spine stiffen. "Ramona, you've got to help me. I must go to him."

That night we staged a daring break. We clubbed the attendant when he brought dinner, and once we had him under the bed we ate all the chops and gluten bread on his cart and then we went down the corridor, lifting bolts, and when we were a hundred strong we locked the matron in her office and raided the dining hall, howling and eating everything we could find. I ate that night, how I ate, but even as I ate I was aware of a fatal lightness in my bones, a failure in capacity, and so they found me in the frozen food locker, weeping over a chain of link sausage, inconsolable because I understood that they had spoiled it for me, they with their chops and their gluten bread; I could never eat as I once had, I would never be myself again.

In my fury I went after the matron with a ham hock, and when I had them all at bay I took a loin of pork for sustenance and I broke out of that place. I had to get to Tommy before I got any thinner; I had to try. Outside the gate I stopped a car and hit the driver with the loin of pork and then I drove to the Hotel Riverside, where Tommy always stayed. I made my way up the fire stairs on little cat feet and when the valet went to his suite with one of his velveteen suits I followed, quick as a tigress, and the next moment I was inside. When all was quiet I tiptoed to his door and stepped inside.

He was magnificent. He stood at the window, gaunt and beautiful; his blond hair fell to his waist and his shoulders shriveled under a heartbreaking double-breasted pea-green velvet suit. He did not see me at first; I drank in his image and then, delicately, cleared my throat. In the second that he turned and saw me, everything seemed possible.

"It's you." His voice throbbed.

"I had to come."

Our eyes fused and in that moment I believed that we two could meet, burning as a single, lambent flame, but in the next second his face had crumpled in disappointment; he brought a picture from his pocket, a fingered, cracked photograph, and he looked from it to me and back at the photograph, saying, "My darling, you've fallen off."

"Maybe it's not too late," I cried, but we both knew I would fail.

And fail I did, even though I ate for days, for five desperate, heroic weeks; I threw pies into the breach, fresh hams and whole sides of beef, but those sad days at the food farm, the starvation and the drugs have so upset my chemistry that it cannot be restored; no matter what I eat I fall off and I continue to fall off; my body is a halfway house for foods I can no longer assimilate. Tommy watches, and because he knows he almost had me, huge and round and beautiful, Tommy mourns. He eats less and less now. He eats like a bird and lately he has refused to sing; strangely, his records have begun to disappear.

And so a whole nation waits.

"I almost had her," he says, when they beg him to resume his midnight shows; he will not sing, he won't talk, but his hands describe the mountain of woman he has longed for all his life.

And so I have lost Tommy, and he has lost me, but I am doing my best to make it up to him. I own Faircrest now, and in the place where Ramona and I once suffered I use my skills on the girls Tommy wants me to cultivate. I can put twenty pounds on a girl in a couple of weeks and I don't mean bloat, I mean solid fat. Ramona and I feed them up and once a week we weigh and I poke the upper arm with a special stick and I will not be satisfied until the stick goes in and does not rebound because all resiliency is gone. Each week I bring out my best and Tommy shakes his head in misery because the best is not yet good enough, none of them are what I once was. But one day the time and the girl will be right—would that it were me—the time and the girl will be right and Tommy will sing again. In the meantime, the whole world waits; in the meantime, in a private wing well away from the others, I keep my special cases; the matron, who grows fatter as I watch her. And Mom. And Dad.

Songs of War

For some weeks now a fire had burned day and night on a hillside just beyond the town limits; standing at her kitchen sink, Sally Hall could see the smoke rising over the trees. It curled upward in promise, but she could not be sure what it promised, and despite the fact that she was contented with her work and her family, Sally found herself stirred by the bright autumn air, the smoke emblem.

Nobody seemed to want to talk much about the fire, or what it meant. Her husband Jack passed it off with a shrug, saying it was probably just another commune. June Goodall, her neighbor, said it was coming from Ellen Ferguson's place, she owned the land and it was her business what she did with it. Sally said what if she had been taken prisoner. Vic Goodall said not to be ridiculous, if Ellen Ferguson wanted those people off her place, all she had to do was call the police and get them off, and in the meantime, it was nobody's business.

Still there was something commanding about the presence of the fire; the smoke rose steadily and could be seen for miles, and Sally, working at her drawing board, and a number of other women, going about their daily business, found themselves yearning after the smoke column with complex feelings. Some may have been recalling a primal past in which men conked large animals and dragged them into camp, and the only housework involved was a little gutting before they roasted the bloody chunks over the fire. The grease used to sink into the dirt and afterward the diners, smeared with blood and fat, would roll around in a happy tangle. Other women were stirred by all the adventure tales they had stored up from childhood; people used to run away without even bothering to pack or leave a note, they always found food one way or another and they met new friends in the woods. Together they would tell stories over a campfire, and when they had eaten they would walk away from the bones to some high excitement which had nothing to do with the business of living from day to day. A few women, thinking of Castro and his happy guerrilla band, in the carefree, glamorous days before he came to power, were closer to the truth. Thinking wistfully of campfire camaraderie, of everybody marching together in a common cause, they were already dreaming of revolution.

Despite the haircut and the cheap suit supplied by the Acme Vacuum Cleaner company, Andy Ellis was an under-achiever college dropout who couldn't care less about vacuum cleaners. Until this week he had been a beautiful, carefree kid, and now, with a dying mother to support, with the wraiths of unpaid bills and unsold Marvelvacs trailing behind him like Marley's chains, he was still beautiful, which is why the women opened their doors to him.

He was supposed to say, "Good morning, I'm from the Acme Vacuum Cleaner Company and I'm here to clean your living room, no obligation, absolutely free of charge." Then, with the room clean and the Marvelsweep with twenty attachments and ten optional features spread all over the rug, he was supposed to make his pitch.

The first woman he called on said he did good work but her husband would have to decide, so Andy sighed and began collecting the Flutesnoot, the Miracle Whoosher and all the other attachments and putting them back into the patented Bomb Bay Door.

"Well thanks anyway . . ."

"Oh, thank *you*," she said. He was astounded to discover that she was unbuttoning him here and there.

"Does this mean you want the vacuum after all?"

She covered him with hungry kisses. "Shut up and deal."

At the next house, he began again. "Good morning, I'm from the Acme Vacuum Cleaner Company . . ."

"Never mind that. Come in."

At the third house, he and the lady of the house grappled in the midst of her unfinished novel, rolling here and there between the unfinished tapestry and the unfinished wire sculpture.

"If he would let me alone for a minute I would get some of these things done," she said. "All he ever thinks about is sex."

"If you don't like it, why are we doing this?"

"To get even," she said.

On his second day as a vacuum cleaner salesman, Andy changed his approach. Instead of going into his pitch, he would say, "Want to make it?" By the third day he had refined it to, "If you insist."

Friday his mother died so he was able to turn in his Marvelvac, which he thought was just as well, because he was exhausted and depressed, and, for all his efforts, he had made only one tentative sale, which was contingent upon his picking up the payments in person every week for the next twelve years. Standing over his mother's coffin, he could not for the life of him understand what had happened to women—not good old Mom, who had more or less liked her family and at any rate had died uncomplaining—but the others, all the women in every condition in all the houses he had gone to this week. Why weren't any of them happy?

Up in the hills, sitting around the fire, the women in the vanguard were talking about just that: the vagaries of life, and woman's condition. They had to think it was only that. If they were going to go on, they would have to be able to decide the problem was X, whatever X was. It had to be something they could name, so that, together, they could do something about it.

They were of a mind to free themselves. One of the things was to free themselves of the necessity of being thought of as sexual objects, which turned out to mean only that certain obvious concessions, like lipstick and pretty clothes, had by ukase been done away with. Still, there were those who wore their khakis and bandoliers with a difference. Whether or not they shaved their legs and armpits, whether or not they smelled, the pretty ones were still pretty and the others were not; the ones with good bodies walked in an unconscious pride and the others tried to ignore the differences and settled into their flesh, saying: Now, we are all equal.

There were great disputes as to what they were going to do, and which things they would do first. It was fairly well agreed that although the law said that they were equal, nothing much was changed. There was still the monthly bleeding; Dr. Ora Fessenden, the noted gynaecologist, had showed them a trick which was supposed to take care of all that, but nothing short of surgery or menopause would halt the process altogether; what man had to undergo such indignities? There was still pregnancy, but the women all agreed they were on top of that problem. That left the rest: men still looked down on them, in part because in the main, women were shorter; they were more or less free to pursue their careers, assuming they could keep a baby sitter, but there were still midafternoon depressions, dishes, the wash; despite all the changes, life was much the same. More drastic action was needed.

They decided to form an army.

At the time, nobody was agreed on what they were going to do or how they would go about it, but they were all agreed that it was time for a change. Things could not go on as they were; life was often boring, and too hard.

"Dear Ralph," she said in her note, "I am running away to realize my full potential. I know you have always said I could do anything I want but what you meant was, I could do anything as long as it didn't mess you up, which is not exactly the same thing now, is it? Don't bother to look for me.

> No longer yours,
> Lory."

Then she went to join the women in the hills.

I would like to go, Suellen thought, *but what if they wouldn't let me have my baby?*

Jolene's uncle in the country always had a liver-colored setter named Fido. The name remained the same and the dogs were more or less interchangeable. Jolene called all her lovers Mike, and because they were more or less interchangeable, eventually she tired of them and went to join the women in the hills.

"You're not going," Herb Chandler said.
Annie said, "I am."
He grabbed her as she reached the door. "The hell you are, I need you."

"You don't need me, you need a maid." She slapped the side of his head. "Now let me go."

"You're mine," he said, aiming a karate chop at her neck. She wriggled and he missed.

"Just like your ox and your ass, huh." She had got hold of a lamp and she let him have it on top of the head.

"Ow," he said, and crumpled to the floor.

"Nobody owns me," she said, throwing the vase of flowers she kept on the side table, just for good measure. "I'll be back when it's over." Stepping over him, she went out of the door.

After everybody left that morning, June mooned around the living room, picking up the scattered newspapers, collecting her and Vic's empty coffee cups and marching out to face the kitchen table, which looked the same way every morning at this time, glossy with spilled milk and clotted cereal, which meant that she had to go through the same motions every morning at this time, feeling more and more like that jerk, whatever his name was, who for eternity kept on pushing the same recalcitrant stone up the hill; he was never going to get it to the top because it kept falling back on him and she was never going to get to the top, wherever that was, because there would always be the kitchen table, and the wash, and the crumbs on the rug, and besides she didn't know where the top was because she had gotten married right after Sweetbriar and the next minute, bang, there was the kitchen table and, give or take a few babies, give or take a few stabs at night classes in something-or-other, that seemed to be her life. There it was in the morning, there it was again at noon, there it was at night; when people said, at parties, "What do you do?" she could only move her hands helplessly because there was no answer she could give which would please either herself or them. *I clean the kitchen table*, she thought, because there was no other way to describe it. Occasionally she thought about running away, but where would she go, and how would she live? Besides, she would miss Vic and the kids and her favorite chair in the television room. Sometimes she thought she might grab the milkman or the next delivery boy, but she knew she would be too embarrassed, either that or she would start laughing, or the delivery boy would, and even if they didn't, she would never be able to face Vic. She thought she had begun to disappear, like the television or the washing machine, after a while nobody would see her at all. They might complain if she wasn't working properly, but in the main she was just another household appliance, and so she mooned, wondering if this was all there was ever going to be: herself in the house, the kitchen table.

Then the notice came.

JOIN NOW

It was in the morning mail, hastily mimeographed and addressed to her by name. If she had been in a different mood she might have tossed it out with the rest of the junk mail, or called a few of her friends to see if they had gotten it too. As it was, she read it through, chewing over certain catchy phrases in this call to arms, surprised to find her blood quickening. Then she packed and wrote her note:

"Dear Vic,

"There are clean sheets on all the beds and three casseroles in the freezer and one in the oven. The veal one should do for two meals. I have done all the wash and a thorough vacuuming. If Sandy's cough doesn't get any better you should take him in to see Dr. Weixelbaum, and don't forget Jimmy is supposed to have his braces tightened on the 12th. Don't look for me.

Love,
June."

Then she went to join the women in the hills.

• • •

Glenda Thompson taught psychology at the university; it was the semester break and she thought she might go to the women's encampment in an open spirit of inquiry. If she liked what they were doing she might chuck Richard, who was only an instructor while she was an assistant professor, and join them. To keep the appearance of objectivity, she would take notes.

Of course she was going to have to figure out what to do with the children while she was gone. No matter how many hours she and Richard taught, the children were her responsibility, and if they were both working in the house, she had to leave her typewriter and shush the children because of the way Richard got when he was disturbed. None of the sitters she called could come; Mrs. Birdsall, their regular sitter, had taken off without notice again, to see her son the freshman in Miami, and she exhausted the list of student sitters without any luck. She thought briefly of leaving them at Richard's office, but she couldn't trust him to remember them at the end of the day. She reflected bitterly that men who wanted to work just got up and went to the office. It had never seemed fair.

"Oh hell," she said finally, and because it was easier, she packed Tommy and Bobby and took them along.

Marva and Patsy and Betts were sitting around in Marva's room; it was two days before the junior prom and not one of them had a date, or even a nibble; there weren't even any blind dates to be had.

"I know what let's do," Marva said, "let's go up to Ferguson's and join the women's army."

Betts said, "I didn't know they had an *army*."

"Nobody knows what they have up there," Patsy said.

They left a note so Marva's mother would be sure and call them in case somebody asked for a date at the last minute and they got invited to the prom after all.

• • •

Sally felt a twinge of guilt when she opened the flier:
JOIN NOW

After she read it she went to the window and looked at the smoke column in open disappointment: *Oh, so that's all it is*. Yearning after it in the early autumn twilight, she had thought it might represent something more: excitement, escape, but she supposed she should have guessed. There was no great getaway, just a bunch of people who needed more people to help. She knew she probably ought to go up and help out for a while, she could design posters and ads they could never afford if they went to a regular graphics studio. Still, all those women . . . She couldn't bring herself to make the first move.

"I'm not a joiner," she said aloud, but that wasn't really it; she had always worked at home, her studio took up one wing of the house and she made her own hours; when she tired of working she could pick at the breakfast dishes or take a nap on the lumpy couch at one end of the studio; when the kids came home she was always there and besides, she didn't like going places without Zack.

Instead she used the flier to test her colors, dabbing blues here, greens there, until she had more or less forgotten the message and all the mimeographing was obscured by color.

At the camp, Dr. Ora Fessenden was leading an indoctrination program for new recruits. She herself was in the stirrups, lecturing coolly while everybody filed by.

One little girl, lifted up by her mother, began to whisper: "Ashphasphazzzzz-pzz."

The mother muttered, "Mumumumummm-mmmm. . . ."

Ellen Ferguson, who was holding the light, turned it on the child for a moment. "Well, what does *she* want?"

"She wants to know what a man's looks like."

Dr. Ora Fessenden took hold, barking from the stirrups. "With luck, she'll never have to see."

"Right on," the butch sisters chorused, but the others began to look at one another in growing discomfiture, which as the weeks passed would ripen into alarm.

By the time she reached the camp, June was already worried about the casseroles she had left for Vic and the kids. Would the one she had left in the oven go bad at room temperature? Maybe she ought to call Vic and tell him to let it bubble for an extra half-hour just in case. Would Vic really keep an eye on Sandy, and if she got worse, would he get her to the doctor in time? What about Jimmy's braces? She almost turned back.

But she was already at the gate to Ellen Ferguson's farm, and she was surprised to see a hastily constructed guardhouse, with Ellen herself in khakis, standing with a carbine at the ready, and she said, "Don't shoot, Ellen, it's me."

"For God's sake, June, I'm not going to shoot you." Ellen pushed her glasses up on her forehead so she could look into June's face. "I never thought you'd have the guts."

"I guess I needed a change."

"Isn't it thrilling?"

"I feel funny without the children." June was trying to remember when she had last seen Ellen: over a bridge table? At Weight Watchers? "How did you get into this?"

"I needed something to live for," Ellen said.

By that time two other women with rifles had impounded her car and then she was in a jeep bouncing up the dirt road to headquarters. The women behind the table all had on khakis, but they looked not at all alike in them. One was tall and tawny and called herself Sheena; there was a tough, funny-looking one named Rap and the third was Margy, still redolent of the kitchen sink. Sheena made the welcoming speech, and then Rap took her particulars while Margy wrote everything down.

She lied a little about her weight, and was already on the defensive when Rap looked at her over her glasses, saying, "Occupation?"

"Uh, household manager."

"Oh shit, another housewife. Skills?"

"Well, I used to paint a little, and..."

Rap snorted.

"I'm pretty good at conversational French."

"Kitchen detail," Rap said to Margy and Margy checked off a box and flipped over to the next sheet.

"But I'm tired of all that," June said.

Rap said, "Next."

Oh it was good sitting around the campfire, swapping stories about the men at work and the men at home, every woman had a horror story, because even the men who claimed to be behind them weren't really behind them, they were paying lip service to avoid a higher price, and even the best among them would make those terrible verbal slips. It was good to talk to other women who were smarter than their husbands and tired of having to pretend they weren't. It was good to be able to sprawl in front of the fire without having to think about Richard and what time he would be home. The kids were safely stashed down at the day care compound, along with everybody else's kids, and for the first time in at least eight years Glenda could relax and think about herself. She listened drowsily to that night's speeches, three examples of wildly diverging cant, and she would have taken notes except that she was full, digesting a dinner she hadn't had to cook, and for almost the first time in eight years she wasn't going to have to go out to the kitchen and face the dishes.

Marva, Patsy and Betts took turns admiring each

other in their new uniforms and they sat at the edge of the group, hugging their knees and listening in growing excitement. Why, they didn't *have* to worry about what they looked like, that wasn't going to matter in the new scheme of things. It didn't *matter* whether or not they had dates. By the time the new order was established, they weren't even going to *want* dates. Although they would rather die than admit it, they all felt a little pang at this. Goodbye hope chest, goodbye wedding trip to Nassau and picture in the papers in the long white veil. Patsy, who wanted to be a corporation lawyer, thought: Why can't I have it *all*.

Now that his mother was dead and he didn't need to sell vacuum cleaners any more, Andy Ellis was thrown back on his own resources. He spent three hours in the shower and three days sleeping, and on the fourth day he emerged to find out his girl had left him for the koto player from across the hall. "Well shit," he said, and wandered into the street.

He had only been asleep for three days but everything was subtly different. The people in the corner market were mostly men, stocking up on TV dinners and chunky soups or else buying cooking wines and herbs, kidneys, beef liver and tripe. The usual girl was gone from the checkout counter, the butcher was running the register instead, and when Andy asked about it, Freddy the manager said, "She joined up."

"Are you kidding?"

"Some girl scout camp up at Ferguson's. The tails' revolt."

Just then a jeep sped by in the street outside, there was a crash and they both hit the floor, rising to their elbows after the object which had shattered the front window did not explode. It was a rock with a note attached. Andy picked his way through the glass to retrieve it. It read:

WE WILL BURY YOU

"See?" Freddy said, ugly and vindictive. "See? See?"

The local hospital admitted several cases of temporary blindness in men who had been attacked by women armed with deodorant spray.

All over town the men whose wives remained lay next to them in growing unease. Although they all feigned sleep, they were aware that the stillness was too profound: the women were thinking.

The women trashed a porn movie house. Among them was the wife of the manager, who said, as she threw an open can of film over the balcony, watching it unroll, "I'm doing this for us."

So it had begun. For the time being, Rap and her cadre, who were in charge of the military operation, intended to satisfy themselves with guerrilla tactics; so far, nobody had been able to link the sniping and *materiel* bombing with the women on the hill, but they all knew it was only a matter of time before the first police cruiser came up to Ellen Ferguson's gate with a search warrant, and they were going to have to wage open war.

By this time one of the back pastures had been converted to a rifle range, and even poor June had to spend at least one hour of every day in practice. She began to take an embarrassing pleasure in it, thinking, as she potted away:

Aha, Vic, there's a nick in your scalp. Maybe you'll remember what I look like next time you leave the house for the day.

OK, kids, I am not the maid.

All right, Sally, you and your damn career. You're still only the maid.

Then, surprisingly: *This is for you, Sheena. How dare*

you go around looking like that, when I have to look like this.

This is for every rapist on the block.

By the time she fired her last shot her vision was blurred by tears. *June you are stupid, stupid, you always have been and you know perfectly well nothing is going to make any difference.*

Two places away, Glenda saw Richard's outline in the target. She made a bull's-eye. *All right, damn you, pick up that toilet brush.*

Going back to camp in the truck they all sang "Up Women" and "The Internacionale," and June began to feel a little better. It reminded her of the good old days at camp in middle childhood, when girls and boys played together as if there wasn't any difference. She longed for that old androgynous body, the time before sexual responsibility. Sitting next to her on the bench, Glenda sang along but her mind was at the university; she didn't know what she was going to do if she got the Guggenheim because Richard had applied without success for so long that he had given up trying. What should she do, lie about it? It would be in all the papers. She wondered how convincing she would be, saying, Shit, honey, it doesn't mean anything. She would have to give up the revolution and get back to her work; her book was only half-written; she would have to go back to juggling kids and house and work; it was going to be hard, hard. She decided finally that she would let the Guggenheim Foundation make the decision for her. She would wait until late February and then write and tell Richard where to forward her mail.

Leading the song, Rap looked at her group. Even the softest ones had callouses now, but it was going to be some time before she made real fighters out of them. She wondered why women had all buried the instinct to kill. It was those damn babies, she decided: grunt, strain, pain, BABY. Hand a mother a gun and tell her to kill and she will say, After I went to all that trouble?

Well if you are going to make sacrifices you are going to have to make sacrifices, she thought, and led them in a chorus of the battle anthem, watching to see just who did and who didn't throw herself into the last chorus, which ended: Kill, kill, *kill*.

Sally was watching the smoke again. Zack said, "I wish you would come away from that window."

She kept looking for longer than he would have liked her to, and when she turned, she said, "Zack, why did you marry me?"

"Couldn't live without you."

"No, really."

"Because I wanted to love you and decorate you and take care of you for the rest of your life."

"Why me?"

"I thought we could be friends for a long time."

"I guess I didn't mean why did you marry *me*, I meant, why did you *marry* me."

He looked into his palms, "I wanted you to take care of me too."

"Is that all?"

He could see she was serious and because she was not going to let go he thought for a minute and said at last, "Nobody wants to die alone."

Down the street, June Goodall's husband Vic had called every hospital in the county without results. The police had no reports of middle-aged housewives losing their memory in Sears or getting raped, robbed or poleaxed anywhere within the city limits. The police sergeant said, "Mr. Goodall, we've got more serious things on our minds, these bombings, for one thing, and the leaflets and the rip-offs. Do you know that women have been walking out of supermarkets with full shopping carts without paying a cent?" There seemed to be a thousand cases like June's, and if the department ever got a minute, it would be first come first served.

So Vic languished in his darkening house. He had managed to get the kids off to school by himself the past couple of days, he gave them money for hot lunches but they were running out of clean clothes and he could not bring himself to sort through those disgusting smelly things in the clothes hamper to run a load of wash. They had run through June's casseroles and they were going to have to start eating out; they would probably go to the Big Beef Plaza tonight, and have pizza tomorrow and chicken the next night and Chinese the next, and if June wasn't back by that time he didn't know what he was going to do because he was at his wits' end. The dishes were piling up in the kitchen and he couldn't understand why everything looked so grimy; he couldn't quite figure out why, but the toilet had begun to smell. One of these days he was going to have to try and get his mother over to clean things up a little. It was annoying, not having any clean underwear. He wished June would come back.

For the fifth straight day, Richard Thompson, Glenda's husband, opened *The French Chef* to a new recipe and prepared himself an exquisite dinner. Once it was finished he relaxed in the blissful silence. Now that Glenda was gone he was able to keep things the way he liked them, he didn't break his neck on Matchbox racers every time he went to put a little Vivaldi on the record player. It was refreshing not to have to meet Glenda's eyes, where, to his growing dissatisfaction, he perpetually measured himself. Without her demands, without the kids around to distract him, he would be able to finish his monograph on Lyly's *Euphues*. He might even begin to write his book. Setting aside Glenda's half-finished manuscript with a certain satisfaction, he cleared a space for himself at the desk and tried to begin.

Castrated, he thought half an hour later. *Her and her damned career, she has castrated me.*

He went to the phone and began calling names on his secret list. For some reason most of them weren't home, but on the fifth call he came up with Jennifer, the biology major who wanted to write poetry, and within minutes the two of them were reaffirming his masculinity on the living-room rug, and if a few pages of Glenda's half-finished manuscript got mislaid in the tussle, who was there to protest? If she was going to be off there, farting around in the woods with all those women, she never would get it finished.

In the hills, the number of women had swelled, and it was apparent to Sheena, Ellen and Rap that it was time to stop hit-and-run terrorism and operate on a larger scale. They would mount a final recruiting campaign. Once that was completed, they would be ready to take their first objective. Sheena had decided the Sunnydell Shopping Center would be their base for a sweep of the entire country. They were fairly sure retaliation would be slow, and to impede it further, they had prepared an advertising campaign built on the slogan: YOU WOULDN'T SHOOT YOUR MOTHER, WOULD YOU? As soon as they could, they would co-opt some television equipment and make their first nationwide telecast from Sunnydell. Volunteers would flock in from fifty states and in time, the country would be theirs.

There was some difference of opinion as to what they were going to do with it. Rap was advocating a scorched-earth policy; the women would rise like phoenixes from the ashes and build a new nation from the rubble, more or less alone. Sheena raised the idea of an auxiliary made up of male sympathizers. The women would rule, but with men at hand. Margy secretly felt that both Rap and Sheena were too militant; she didn't want things to be completely different, only a little better. Ellen Ferguson wanted to annex all the land surrounding her place. She envisioned it as the capitol city of the new world. The butch sisters wanted special legislation which would outlaw contact, social or sexual, with men, with, perhaps, special provisions for social meetings with their gay brethren. Certain of the straight sisters were made uncomfortable by their association with the butch sisters and wished there were some way the battle could progress without them. At least half of these women wanted their men back, once victory was assured, and the other half were looking into ways of perpetuating the race by means of parthenogenesis, or, at worst, sperm banks and AI techniques. One highly vocal splinter group wanted mandatory sterilization for everybody, and a portion of the lunatic fringe was demanding transsexual operations. Because nobody could agree, the women decided for the time being to skip over the issues and concentrate on the war effort itself.

By this time, word had spread and the volunteers were coming in, so it was easy to ignore issues because logistics were more pressing. It was still warm enough for the extras to bunk in the fields, but winter was coming on and the women were going to have to manage food, shelters and uniforms for an unpredictable number. There had been a temporary windfall when Rap's bunch hijacked a couple of semis filled with frozen dinners and surplus clothes, but Rap and Sheena and the others could sense the hounds of hunger and need not far away and so they worked feverishly to prepare for the invasion. Unless they could take the town by the end of the month, they were lost.

"We won't have to hurt our *fathers*, will we?" Although she was now an expert marksman and had been placed in charge of a platoon, Patsy was still not at ease with the cause.

Rap avoided her eyes, "Don't be ridiculous."

"I just couldn't do that to anybody I *loved*," Patsy said. She reassembled her rifle, driving the bolt into place with a click.

"Don't you worry about it," Rap said. "All you have to worry about is looking good when you lead that recruiting detail."

"OK." Patsy tossed her hair. She knew how she and her platoon looked, charging into the wind; she could feel the whole wild group around her, on the run with their heads high and their bright hair streaming. *I wish the boys at school could see*, she thought, and turned away before Rap could guess what she was thinking.

I wonder if any woman academic can be happy. Glenda was on latrine detail and this always made her reflective. *Maybe if they marry garage mechanics.* In the old days there had been academic types: single, tweedy, sturdy in orthopedic shoes, but somewhere along the way these types had been supplanted by married women of every conceivable type, who pressed forward in wildly varied disciplines, having in common only the singular harried look which marked them all. The rubric was more or less set: if you were good, you always had to worry about whether you were short-changing your family; if you weren't as good as he was, you would always have to wonder whether it was because of all the other duties: babies, meals, the house; if despite everything you turned out to be better than he was, then you had to decide whether to try and minimize it, or prepare yourself for the wise looks on the one side, on the other, his look of uncomprehending reproach. If you *were* better than he was, then why should you be wasting your time with *him*? She felt light years removed from the time when girls used to be advised to let *him* win the tennis match; everybody played to win now, but she had the uncomfortable feeling that there might never be any real victories. Whether or not you won, there were too many impediments: if he had a job and you didn't, then tough; if you both had jobs but he didn't get tenure, then you had to quit and move with him to a new place. She poured Lysol into the last toilet and turned her back on it, thinking: *Maybe that's why those Hollywood marriages are always breaking up.*

Sally finished putting the children to bed and came back into the living room, where Zack was waiting for her on the couch. By this time she had heard the women's broadcasts, she was well aware of what was going on at Ellen Ferguson's place and knew as well that this was where June was, and June was so inept, so soft and incapable that she really ought to be up there helping June, helping *them*; it was a job that ought to be done, on what scale she could not be sure, but the fire was warm and Zack was waiting; he and the children, her career, were all more important than that abstraction in the hills; she had negotiated her own peace—let them take care of theirs. Settling in next to Zack, she thought: *I don't love my little pink dishmop, I don't, but everybody has to shovel* some *shit.* Then: *God help the sailors and poor fishermen who have to be abroad on a night like this.*

June had requisitioned a jeep and was on her way into town to knock over the corner market, because food was already in short supply. She had on the housedress she had worn when she enlisted, and she would carry somebody's old pink coat over her arm to hide the pistol and the grenade she would use to hold her hostages at bay while the grocery boys filled up the jeep. She had meant to go directly to her own corner market, thinking, among other things, that the manager might recognize her and tell Vic, after which, of course, he would track her back to the camp and force her to come home to him and the children. Somehow or other she went right by the market and ended up at the corner of her street.

She knew she was making a mistake but she parked

and began to prowl the neighborhood. The curtains in Sally's window were drawn but the light behind them gave out a rosy glow which called up in her longings which she could not have identified; they had very little to do with her own home, or her life with Vic; they dated, rather from her childhood, when she had imagined marriage, had prepared herself for it with an amorphous but unshakeable idea of what it would be like.

Vic had forgotten to put out the garbage; overflowing cans crowded the back porch and one of them was overturned. Walking on self-conscious cat feet, June made her way up on the porch and peered into the kitchen: just as she had suspected, a mess. A portion of her was tempted to go in and do a swift, secret cleaning; *The phantom housewife STRIKES*, but the risk of being discovered was too great. Well let him clean up his own damn messes from now on. She tiptoed back down the steps and went around the house, crunching through bushes to look into the living room. She had hoped to get a glimpse of the children, but they were already in bed. She thought about waking Juney with pebbles on her window, whispering: Don't worry, mother's all right; but she wasn't strong enough; if she saw the children she would never be able to walk away and return to camp. She assuaged herself by thinking she would come back for Juney and Victor Junior just as soon as victory was assured. The living room had an abandoned look, with dust visible and papers strewn, a chair overturned and Vic himself asleep on the couch, just another neglected object in this neglected house. Surprised at how little she felt, she shrugged and turned away. On her way back to the jeep she did stop to right the garbage can.

The holdup went off all right; she could hear distant sirens building behind her, but so far as she knew, she wasn't followed.

The worst thing turned out to be finding Rap, Sheena and Ellen Ferguson gathered around the stove in the main cabin; they didn't hear her come in.

". . . so damn fat and soft," Rap was saying.

Sheena said, "You have to take your soldiers where you can find them."

Ellen said, "An army travels on its stomach."

"As soon as it's over we dump the housewives," Rap said. "Every single one."

June cleared her throat. "I've brought the food."

"Politics may make strange bedfellows," Glenda said, "but this is ridiculous."

"Have it your way," she said huffily—whoever she was—and left the way she came.

Patsy was in charge of the recruiting platoon which visited the high school, and she thought the principal was really impressed when he saw that it was her. Her girls bound and gagged the faculty and held the boys at bay with M-Is, while she made her pitch. She was successful but drained when she finished, pale and exhausted, and while her girls were processing the recruits (all but one percent of the girl students, as it turned out) and waiting for the bus to take them all to camp, Patsy put Marva in charge and simply drifted away, surprised to find herself in front of the sweet shop two blocks from school. The place was empty except for Andy Ellis, who had just begun work as a counter boy.

He brought her a double dip milkshake and lingered.

She tried to wave him away with her rifle. "We don't have to pay."

"That isn't it." He yearned, drawn to her.

She couldn't help seeing how beautiful he was. "Bug off."

Andy said, "Beautiful."

She lifted her head, aglow. "Really?"

"No kidding. Give me a minute, I'm going to fall in love with you."

"You can't," she said, remembering her part in the eleventh grade production of *Romeo and Juliet*. "I'm some kind of Montague."

"OK, then, I'll be the Capulet."

"I . . ." Patsy leaned forward over the counter so they could kiss. She drew back at the sound of a distant shot. "I have to go."

"When can I see you?"

Patsy said, "I'll sneak out tonight."

Sheena was in charge of the recruiting detail which visited Sally's neighborhood. Although she had been an obscure first-year medical student when the upheaval started, she was emerging as the heroine of the revolution. The newspapers and television newscasters all knew who she was, and so Sally knew, and was undeniably flattered that she had come.

She and Sally met on a high level: if there was an aristocracy of achievement, then they spoke aristocrat to aristocrat. Sheena spoke of talent and obligation; she spoke of need and duty; she spoke of service. She said the women needed Sally's help, and when Sally said, Let them help themselves, she said: They can't. They were still arguing when the kids came home from school; they were still arguing when Zack came home. Sheena spoke of the common cause and a better world; she spoke once more of the relationship between talent and service. Sally turned to Zack, murmuring, and he said:

"If you think you have to do it, then I guess you'd better do it."

She said: "The sooner I go the sooner it'll be over."

Zack said, "I hope you're right."

Sheena stood aside so they could make their goodbyes. Sally hugged the children, and when they begged to go with her she said, "It's no place for kids."

Climbing into the truck, she looked back at Zack and thought: *I could not love thee half so much loved I not honor more.* What she said was, "I must be out of my mind."

Zack stood in the street with his arms around the kids, saying, "She'll be back soon. Some day they'll come marching down our street."

In the truck, Sheena said, "Don't worry. When we occupy, we'll see that he gets a break."

They were going so fast now that there was no jumping off the truck; the other women at the camp seemed to be so grateful to see her that she knew there would be no jumping off the truck until it was over.

June whispered: "To be perfectly honest, I was beginning to have my doubts about the whole thing, but with *you* along . . ."

They made her a member of the council.

The next day the women took the Sunnydell Shopping Center, which included two supermarkets, a discount house, a fast food place and a cinema; they selected it because it was close to camp and they could change guard details with a minimum of difficulty. The markets would solve the food problem for the time being, at least.

In battle, they used M-Is, one submachine-gun and a variety of sidearms and grenades. They took the place without firing a shot.

The truth was that until this moment, the men had not taken the revolution seriously.

The men had thought: After all, it's only women.

They had thought: Let them have their fun. We can stop this thing whenever we like.

They had thought: What difference does it make? They'll come crawling back to us.

In this first foray, the men, who were, after all, unarmed, fled in surprise. Because the women had not been able to agree upon policy, they let their vanquished enemy go; for the time being, they would take no prisoners.

They were sitting around the victory fire that night, already aware that it was chilly and when the flames burned down a bit they were going to have to go back inside. It was then, for the first time, that Sheena raised the question of allies.

She said, "Sooner or later we have to face facts. We can't make it alone."

Sally brightened, thinking of Zack: "I think you're right."

Rap leaned forward. "Are you *serious*?"

Sheena tossed her hair. "What's the matter with sympathetic men?"

"The only sympathetic man is a dead man," Rap said.

Sally rose. "Wait a minute..."

Ellen Ferguson pulled her down. "Relax. All she means is, at this stage we can't afford any risks. Infiltration. Spies."

Sheena said, "We could use a few men."

Sally heard herself, *sotto voce*: "You're not kidding."

Dr. Ora Fessenden rose, in stages. She said, with force: "Look here, Sheena, if you are going to take a stance, you are going to have to take a stance."

If she had been there, Patsy would have risen to speak in favor of a men's auxiliary. As it was, she had sneaked out to meet Andy. They were down in the shadow of the conquered shopping center, falling in love.

In the command shack, much later, Sheena paced moodily. "They aren't going to be satisfied with the shopping center for long."

Sally said, "I think things are going to get out of hand."

"They can't," Sheena kept on pacing. "We have too much to do."

"Your friend Rap and the doctor are out for blood. Lord knows how many of the others are going to go along." Sally sat at the desk, doodling on the roll sheet. "Maybe you ought to dump them."

"We need muscle, Sally."

Margy, who seemed to be dusting, said, "I go along."

"No." Lory was in the corner, transcribing Sheena's remarks of the evening. "Sheena's absolutely right."

It was morning, and Ellen Ferguson paced the perimeter of the camp. "We're going to need fortifications here, and more over here."

Glenda, who followed with the clipboard, said, "What are you expecting?"

"I don't know, but I want to be ready for it."

"Shouldn't we be concentrating on *off*ense?"

"Not me," Ellen said, with her feet set wide in the dirt. "This is my place. This is where I make my stand."

"Allies. That woman is a marshmallow. *Allies*." Rap was still seething. "I think we ought to go ahead and make our play."

"We still need them," Dr. Ora Fessenden said. The two of them were squatting in the woods above the camp. "When we get strong enough, then . . ." She drew her finger across her throat. "Zzzzt."

"Dammit to hell, Ora." Rap was on her feet, punching a tree trunk. "If you're going to fight, you're going to have to kill."

"You know it and I know it," Dr. Ora Fessenden said. "Now try and tell that to the rest of the girls."

As she settled into the routine, Sally missed Zack more and more, and, partly because she missed him so much, she began making a few inquiries. The consensus was that women had to free themselves from every kind of dependence, both emotional and physical; sexual demands would be treated on the level of other bodily functions: any old toilet would do.

"Hello, Ralph?"
"Yes?"
"It's me, Lory. Listen, did you read about what we did?"
"About what *who* did?"
"Stop trying to pretend you don't know. Ralph, that was us that took over out at Sunnydale. *Me*."
"You and what army?"
"The women's army. Oh, I see, you're being sarcastic. Well listen, Ralph, I said I was going to realize myself as a person and I have. I'm a sub-lieutenant now. A sub-lieutenant, imagine."
"What about your novel you were going to write about your rotten marriage?"
"Don't pick nits. I'm Sheena's secretary now. You were holding me back, Ralph, all those years you were dragging me down. Well now I'm a free agent. Free."
"Terrific."
"Look, I have to go; we have uniform inspection now and worst luck, I drew K.P."

"Listen," Rap was saying to a group of intent women, "You're going along minding your own business and WHAM, he swoops down like the wolf upon the fold. It's the ultimate weapon."

Dr. Ora Fessenden said, bitterly, "And you just try and rape him back."

Margy said, "I thought men were, you know, supposed to protect women from all that."

Annie Chandler, who had emerged as one of the militants, threw her knife into a tree. "Try and convince them it ever happened. The cops say you must have led him on."

Dr. Ora Fessenden drew a picture of the woman as ruined city, with gestures.

"I don't know what I would do if one of them tried to . . ." Betts said to Patsy. "What would you do?"

Oh Andy. Patsy said, "I don't know."

"There's only one thing *to* do," Rap said, with force. "Shoot on sight."

It was hard to say what their expectations had been after their first victory. There were probably almost as many expectations as there were women. A certain segment of the group was disappointed because Vic/Richard/Tom-Dick-Harry had not come crawling up the hill, crying, My God how I have misused you, Come home and everything will be different. Rap and the others would have wished for more carnage, and as the days passed the thirst for blood heaped dust in their mouths; Sheena was secretly disappointed that there had not been wider coverage of the battle in the press and on nationwide TV. The mood in the camp after that first victory was one of anticlimax, indefinable but growing discontent, *cafard*.

Petty fights broke out in the rank-and-file.

There arose, around this time, some differences between the rank-and-file women, some of whom had children, and the Mothers' Escadrille, an elite corps of women who saw themselves as professional mothers. As a group, they looked down on people like Glenda, who sent their children off to the day care compound. The Mothers' Escadrille would admit, when pressed, that their goal in banding together was the eventual elimination of the role of the man in the family, for man, with his incessant demands, interfered with the primary function of the Mother. Still, they had to admit that, since they had no other profession, they were going to have to be assured some kind of financial support in the ultimate scheme of things. They also wanted more respect from the other women, who seemed to look down on them because they lacked technical or professional skills, and so they conducted their allotted duties in a growing atmosphere of hostility.

It was after a heated discussion with one of the Mothers that Glenda, suffering guilt pangs and feelings of inadequacy, went down to the day care compound to see her own children. She picked them out at once, playing in the middle of a tangle of pre-schoolers, but she saw with a pang that Bobby was reluctant to leave the group to come and talk to her, and even after she said, "It's Mommy," it took Tommy a measurable number of seconds before he recognized her.

The price, she thought in some bitterness. *I hope in the end it turns out to be worth the price.*

Betts had tried running across the field both with and without her bra, and except for the time when she wrapped herself in the Ace bandage, she definitely bounced. At the moment nobody in the camp was agreed as to whether it was a good or a bad thing to bounce; it was either another one of those things the world at large was going to have to, by God, learn to ignore, or else it was a sign of weakness. Either way, it was uncomfortable, but so was the Ace bandage uncomfortable.

Sally was drawn towards home but at the same time, looking around at the disparate women and their growing discontentment, she knew she ought to stay on until the revolution had put itself in order. The women were unable to agree what the next step would be, or to consolidate their gains, and so she met late into the night with Sheena, and walked around among the others. She had the feeling she could help, that whatever her own circumstance, the others were so patently miserable that she must help.

"Listen," said Zack, when Sally called him to explain, "it's no picnic being a guy, either."

The fear of rape had become epidemic. Perhaps because there had been no overt assault on the women's camp, no Army battalions, not even any police cruisers, the women expected more subtle and more brutal retaliation. The older women were outraged because some of the younger women said what difference did it make? If you were going to make it, what did the circumstances matter? Still, the women talked about it around the campfire and at last it was agreed that regardless of individual reactions, for ideological reasons it was important that it be made impossible; the propaganda value to the enemy would be too great, and so, at Rap's suggestion, each woman was instructed to carry her handweapon at all times and to shoot first and ask questions later.

Patsy and Andy Ellis were finding more and more ways to be together, but no matter how much they were together, it didn't seem to be enough. Since Andy's hair was long, they thought briefly of disguising him as a woman and getting him into camp, but a number of things: whiskers, figure, musculature, would give him away and Patsy decided it would be too dangerous.

"Look, I'm in love with you," Andy said. "Why don't you run away?"

"Oh, I couldn't do that," Patsy said, trying to hide herself in his arms. "And besides . . ."

He hid his face in her hair. "Besides nothing."

"No, really. Besides. Everybody has guns now, everybody has different feelings, but they all hate deserters. We have a new policy."

"They'd never find us."

She looked into Andy's face. "Don't you want to hear about the new policy?"

"OK, what?"

"About deserters." She spelled it out, more than a little surprised at how far she had come. "It's hunt down and shave and kill."

"They wouldn't really do that."

"We had the first one last night, this poor old lady, about forty? She got homesick for her family and tried to run away."

Andy was still amused. "They shaved all her hair off."

"That wasn't all," Patsy said. "When they got finished they really did it. Firing squad, the works."

Although June would not have been sensitive to it, there were diverging feelings in the camp about who did what, and what there was to do. All she knew was she was sick and tired of working in the day care compound and when she went to Sheena and complained, Sheena, with exquisite sensitivity, put her in charge of the detail guarding the shopping center. It was a temporary assignment but it gave June a chance to put on a cartridge belt and all the other paraphernalia of victory, so she cut an impressive figure for Vic, when he came along.

"It's me, honey, don't you know me?"

"Go away," she said with some satisfaction. "No civilians allowed."

"Oh for God's sake."

To their mutual astonishment, she raised her rifle. "Bug off, fella!"

"You don't really think you can get away with this."

"Bug off or I'll shoot."

"We're just letting you do this, to get it out of your system?" Vic moved as if to relieve her of the rifle. "If it makes you feel a little better . . ."

"This is your last warning."

"Listen," Vic said, a study in male outrage. "One step too far, and, TSCHOOM, federal troops."

She fired a warning shot so he left.

• • •

Glenda was a little sensitive about the fact that various husbands had found ways to smuggle in messages, some had even come looking for their wives, but not Richard. One poor bastard had been shot when he came in too close to the fire; they heard an outcry and a thrashing in the bushes but when they looked for him the next morning there was no body; so he must have dragged himself away. There had been notes in food consignments and one husband had hired a skywriter, but so far she had neither word nor sign from Richard, and she wasn't altogether convinced she cared. He seemed to have drifted off into time past along with her job, her students and her book. Once her greatest hope had been to read her first chapter at the national psychological conference; now she wondered whether there would even be any more conferences. If she and the others were successful, that would break down, along with a number of other things. Still, in the end she would have her definitive work on the woman's revolution, but so far the day-to-day tasks had been so engrossing that she hadn't had a minute to begin. Right now, there was too much to do.

They made their first nationwide telecast from a specially erected podium in front of the captured shopping center. For various complicated reasons the leaders made Sally speak first, and, as they had anticipated, she espoused the moderate view: this was a matter of service, women were going to have to give up a few things to help better the lot of their sisters. Once the job was done everything would be improved, but not really different.

Sheena came next, throwing back her bright hair and issuing the call to arms. The mail she drew would include several spirited letters from male volunteers who were already in love with her and would follow her anywhere; because the woman had pledged never to take allies, these letters would be destroyed before they ever reached her.

Dr. Ora Fessenden was all threats, fire and brimstone. Rap took up where she left off.

"We're going to fight until there's not a man left standing..."

Annie Chandler yelled, "Right on."

Margy was trying to speak: "... just a few concessions..."

Rap's eyes glittered. "Only sisters, and you guys..."

Ellen Ferguson said, "Up, women, out of slavery."

Rap's voice rose. "You guys are going to burn."

Sally was saying, "Reason with you..."

Rap hissed: "Bury you."

It was hard to say which parts of these messages reached the viewing public, as the women all interrupted and overrode each other and the cameraman concentrated on Sheena, who was to become the sign and symbol of the revolution. None of the women on the platform seemed to be listening to any of the others, which may have been just as well; the only reason they had been able to come this far together was because nobody ever did.

The letters began to come:

"Dear Sheena, I would like to join, but I already have nine children and now I am pregnant again..."

"Dear Sheena, I am a wife and mother but I will throw it all over in an instant if you will only glance my way..."

"Dear Sheena, our group has occupied the town hall in Gillespie, Indiana, but we are running out of ammo and the water supply is low. Several of the women have been stricken with plague, and we are running out of food..."

"First I made him lick my boots and then I killed him but now I have this terrible problem with the body, the kids don't want me to get rid of him . . ."

"Who do you think you are running this war when you don't even know what you are doing, what you have to do is kill every last damn one of them and the ones you don't kill you had better cut off their Things . . ."

"Sheena, baby, if you will only give up this halfassed revolution you and I can make beautiful music together, I have signed this letter Maud to escape the censors but if you look underneath the stamp you can see who I really am."

The volunteers were arriving in dozens. The first thing was that there was not housing for all of them; there was not equipment, and so the women in charge had to cut off enlistments at a certain point and send the others back to make war in their own home towns.

The second thing was that, with the increase in numbers, there was an increasing bitterness about the chores. Nobody wanted to do them; in secret truth nobody ever had, but so far the volunteers had all borne it, up to a point, because they sincerely believed that in the new order there would be no chores. Now they understood that the more people there were banded together, the more chores there would be. Laundry and garbage were piling up. At some point around the time of the occupation of the shopping center, the women had begun to understand that no matter what they accomplished, there would always be ugly things to do: the chores, and now, because there seemed to be so *much* work, there were terrible disagreements as to who was supposed to do what, and as a consequence they had all more or less stopped doing any of it.

Meals around the camp were catch as catch can.

The time was approaching when nobody in the camp would have clean underwear.

The latrines were unspeakable.

The children were getting out of hand; some of them were forming packs and making raids of their own, so that the quartermaster never had any clear idea of what she would find in the storehouse. Most of the women in the detail which had been put in charge of the day care compound were fed up.

By this time Sheena was a national figure; her picture was on the cover of both newsmagazines in the same week and there were nationally distributed lines of sweatshirts and tooth glasses bearing her picture and her name. She received love mail and hate mail in such quantity that Lory, who had joined the women to realize her potential as an individual, had to give up her other duties to concentrate on Sheena's mail. She would have to admit that it was better than K.P., and besides, if Sheena went on to better things, maybe she would get to go with her.

The air of dissatisfaction grew. Nobody agreed any more, not even all those who had agreed to agree for the sake of the cause. Fights broke out like flash fires; some women were given to sulks and inexplicable silences, others to blows and helpless tears quickly forgotten. On advice from Sally, Sheena called a council to try and bring everybody together, but it got off on the wrong foot.

Dr. Ora Fessenden said, "Are we going to sit around on our butts, or what?"

Sheena said, "National opinion is running in our favor. We have to consolidate our gains."

Rap said, "Gains hell. What kind of war is this? Where are the scalps?"

Sheena drew herself up. "We are not Amazons."

Rap said, "That's a crock of shit," and she and Dr. Ora Fessenden stamped out.

• • •

"Rape," Rap screamed, running from the far left to the far right and then making a complete circuit of the clearing. "Rape," she shouted, taking careful note of who came running and who didn't. "Raaaaaaaape."

Dr. Ora Fessenden rushed to her side, the figure of outraged womanhood. They both watched until a suitable number of women had assembled, and then she said, in stentorian tones, "We cannot let this go unavenged."

"My God," Sheena said, looking at the blackened object in Rap's hand. "What are you doing with that thing?"

Blood-smeared and grinning, Rap said, "When you're trying to make a point, you have to go ahead and make your point." She thrust her trophy into Sheena's face.

Sheena averted her eyes quickly; she thought it was an ear. "That's supposed to be a *rhetorical* point."

"Listen, baby, this world doesn't give marks for good conduct."

Sheena stiffened. "You keep your girls in line or you're finished."

Rap was smouldering; she pushed her face up to Sheena's, saying, "You can't do without us and you know it."

"If we have to, we'll learn."

"Aieee." One of Rap's cadre had taken the trophy from her and tied it on a string; now she ran through the camp, swinging it around her head, and dozens of throats opened to echo her shout. "Aiiiieeeee . . ."

Patsy and Andy were together in the bushes near the camp; proximity to danger made their pleasure more intense. Andy said:

"Leave with me."

She said, "I can't. I told you what they do to deserters."

"They'll never catch us."

"You don't know these women," Patsy said. "Look, Andy, you'd better go."

"Just a minute more." Andy buried his face in her hair. "Just a little minute more."

"Rape," Rap shouted again, running through the clearing with her voice raised like a Klaxon. "RAAAAAAAAPE."

Although she knew it was a mistake, Sally had sneaked away to see Zack and the children. The camp seemed strangely deserted, and nobody was there to sign out the jeep she took. She had an uncanny intimation of trouble at a great distance but she shook it off and drove to her house. She would have expected barricades and guards: state of war, but the streets were virtually empty and she reached her neighborhood without trouble.

Zack and the children embraced her and wanted to know when she was coming home.

"Soon, I think. They're all frightened of us now."

Zack said, "I'm not so sure."

"There doesn't seem to be any resistance."

"Oh," he said, "they've decided to let you have the town."

"What did I tell you?"

"Sop," he said. "You can have anything you want. Up to a point."

Sally was thinking of Rap and Dr. Ora Fessenden. "What if we take more?"

"Wipeout," Zack said. "You'll see."

"Oh Lord," she said, vaulting into the jeep. "Maybe it'll be over sooner than I thought."

She was already too late. She saw the flames shooting skywards as she came out of the drive.

"It's Flowermont."

Because she had to make sure, she wrenched the jeep

in that direction and rode to the garden apartments; smoke filled the streets for blocks around.

Looking at the devastation, Sally was reminded of Indian massacres in the movies of her childhood: the smoking ruins, the carnage, the moans of the single survivor, who would bubble out his story in her arms. She could not be sure about the bodies: whether there were any, whether there were as many as she thought, but she was sure those were charred corpses in the rubble. Rap and Dr. Ora Fessenden had devised a flag and hoisted it from a tree: the symbol of the women's movement, altered to suit their mood—the crudely executed fist reduced to clenched bones and surrounded by flames. The single survivor died before he could bubble out his story in her arms.

In the camp, Rap and Dr. Ora Fessenden led a victory celebration around the fire. They had taken unspeakable trophies in their raid and could not understand why many of the women refused to wear them.

Patsy and Andy, in the bushes, watched with growing alarm. Even from their safe distance, Andy was fairly sure he saw what he thought he saw, and he whispered, "Look, we've got to get out of here."

"Not now," Patsy said, pulling him closer. "Tonight. The patrols."

By now the little girls had been brought up from the day care compound and they had joined the dance, their fat cheeks smeared with blood. Rap's women were in heated discussion with the Mothers' Escadrille about the disposition of the boy children: would they be destroyed or reared as slaves? While they were talking, one of the mothers who had never felt at home in any faction sneaked down to the compound and freed the lot of them. Now she was running around in helpless tears, flapping her arms and sobbing broken messages, but no matter what she said to the children, she couldn't seem to get any of them to flee.

Sheena and her lieutenant, Margy, and Lory, her secretary, came out of the command shack at the same moment Sally arrived in camp; she rushed to join them, and together they extracted Rap and Dr. Ora Fessenden from the dance for a meeting of the Council.

When they entered the shack, Ellen Ferguson hung up the phone in clattering haste and turned to confront them with a confusing mixture of expressions; Sally thought the foremost one was probably guilt.

Sally waited until they were all silent and then said, "The place is surrounded. Army. National Guard. They let me through to bring the message. They have tanks."

Ellen Ferguson said, "They just delivered their ultimatum. Stop the raids and pull back to camp or they'll have bombers level this place."

"Pull back hell," Rap said.

Dr. Ora Fessenden shook a bloody fist. "We'll show them."

"We'll fight to the death."

Ellen said, quietly, "I've already agreed."

Down at the main gate, Marva, who was on guard duty, leaned across the barbed wire to talk to the captain of the tank detail. She thought he was kind of cute.

"Don't anybody panic," Rap was saying. "We can handle this thing. We can fight them off."

"We can fight them in the hedgerows," Dr. Ora Fessenden said in rising tones. "We can fight them in the ditches, we can hit them with everything we've got . . ."

"Not from here you can't."

"We can burn and bomb and kill and . . . What did you say?"

"I said, not from here." Because they were all staring, Ellen Ferguson covered quickly, saying, "I mean, if I'm going to be of any value to the movement,

I have to have this place in good condition."

Sheena said, quietly, "That's not what you mean."

Ellen was near tears. "All right, dammit, this place is all I have."

"My God," Annie Chandler shrieked. "Rape." She parted the bushes to reveal Patsy and Andy, who hugged each other in silence. "Rape," Annie screamed, and everybody who could hear above the din came running. "Kill the bastard, rape, rape, rape."

Patsy rose to her feet and drew Andy up with her, shouting to make herself heard. "I said, it isn't rape."

Rap and Dr. Ora Fessenden were advancing on Ellen Ferguson. "You're not going to compromise us. We'll kill you first."

"Oh," Ellen said, backing away. "That's another thing. They wanted the two of you. I had to promise we'd send you out."

The two women plunged, and then retreated, mute with fury. Ellen had produced a gun from her desk drawer and now she had them covered.

"Son of a bitch," Rap said. "Son of a bitch."

"Kill them."
"Burn them."
"Hurt them."
"Make an example of them."
"I love you, Patsy."
"Oh, Andy, I love you."

Sally said, softly, "So it's all over."

"Only parts of it," Ellen said. "It will never really be over as long as there are women left to fight. We'll be better off without those two and their cannibals, we can retrench and make a new start."

"I guess this is as good a time as any." Sheena got to her feet. "I might as well tell you, I'm splitting."

They turned to face her, Ellen being careful to keep the gun on Dr. Ora Fessenden and Rap.

"You're what?"

"I can do a hell of a lot more good on my new show. Prime time, nightly, nationwide TV."

Rap snarled. "The hell you say."

"Look, Rap, I'll interview you."

"Stuff it."

"Think what I can do for the movement, I can reach sixty million people, you'll see."

Ellen Ferguson said, with some satisfaction, "That's not really what you mean."

"Maybe it isn't. It's been you, you, you all this time." Sheena picked up her clipboard, her notebooks and papers; Lory and Margy both moved as if to follow her but she rebuffed them with a single sweep of her arm. "Well it's high time I started thinking about me."

Outside, the women had raised a stake and now Patsy and Andy were lashed to it, standing back to back.

In the shack, Rap and Dr. Ora Fessenden had turned as one and advanced on Ellen Ferguson, pushing the gun aside.

The good doctor said, "I knew you wouldn't have the guts to shoot. You never had any guts."

Ellen cried out. "Sheena, help me."

But Sheena was already in the doorway, and she hesitated for only a moment, saying, "Listen, it's *sauve qui peut* in this day and time, sweetie, and the sooner you realize it the better."

Rap finished pushing Ellen down and took the gun. She stood over her victim for a minute, grinning. "In the battle of the sexes, there are no allies." Then she put a bullet through Ellen's favorite moose-head so Ellen would have something to remember her by.

The women had collected twigs and they were just

about to set fire to Patsy and Andy when Sheena came out, closely followed by Dr. Ora Fessenden and a warlike Rap.

Everybody started shouting at once and in the imbroglio that followed, Patsy and Andy escaped. They would surface years later, in a small town in Minnesota, with an ecologically alarming number of children; they would both be able to pursue their chosen careers in the law because they worked hand in hand to take care of all the children and the house, and they would love each other until they died.

Ellen Ferguson sat with her elbows on her knees and her head drooping, saying, "I can't believe it's all over, after I worked so hard, I gave so much . . ."

Sally said, "It isn't over. Remember what you said, as long as there are women, there will be a fight."

"But we've lost our leaders."

"You could . . ."

"No I couldn't."

"Don't worry, there are plenty of others."

As Sally spoke, the door opened and Glenda stepped in to take Sheena's place.

When the mêlée in the clearing was over, Dr. Ora Fessenden and Rap had escaped with their followers. They knew the lay of the land and so they were able to elude the troop concentration which surrounded the camp, and began to lay plans to regroup and fight another day.

A number of women, disgusted by the orgy of violence, chose to pack their things and go. The Mothers' Escadrille deserted *en masse*, taking their children and a few children who didn't even belong to them.

Ellen said, "You're going to have to go down there and parley. I'm not used to talking to men."

And so Sally found herself going down to the gate to conduct negotiations.

She said, "The two you wanted got away. The rest of them—I mean us—are acting in good faith." She lifted her chin. "If you want to go ahead and bomb anyway, you'll have to go ahead and bomb."

The captain lifted her and set her on the hood of the jeep. He was grinning. "Shit, little lady, we just wanted to throw a scare into you."

"You don't understand." She wanted to get down off the hood but he had propped his arms on either side of her. She knew she ought to be furious, but instead she kept thinking how much she missed Zack. Speaking with as much dignity as she could under the circumstances, she outlined the women's complaints; she already knew it was hopeless to list them as demands.

"Don't you worry about a thing, honey." He lifted her down and gave her a slap on the rump to speed her on her way. "Everything is going to be real different from now on."

"I bet."

Coming back up the hill to camp, she saw how sad everything looked and she could not for the life of her decide whether it was because the women who had been gathered here had been inadequate to the cause or whether it was, rather, that the cause itself had been insufficiently identified: she suspected that they had come up against the human condition, failed to recognize it and so tried to attack a single part, which seemed to involve attacking the only allies they would ever have. As for the specific campaign, as far as she could tell, it was possible to change some of the surface or superficial details but once that was done things were still going to be more or less the way they were, and all the best will in the world would not make any real difference.

In the clearing, Lory stood at Glenda's elbow. "Of course you're going to need a lieutenant."

Glenda said, "I guess so."

Ellen Ferguson was brooding over a row of birches which had been leveled during the struggle. If she could stake them back up in time, they might re-root.

June said, "OK, I'm going to be mess sergeant."
Margy said, "The hell you will," and pushed her in the face.

Glenda said, thoughtfully, "Maybe we could mount a Lysistrata campaign."
Lory snorted. "If their wives won't do it, there are plenty of girls who will."

Zack sent a message:
    WE HAVE TO HELP EACH OTHER
Sally sent back: I KNOW.

Before she went home, Sally had to say goodbye to Ellen Ferguson.
Ellen's huge, homely face sagged. "Not you too."
Sally looked at the desultory groups policing the wreckage, at the separate councils convening in every corner. "I don't know why I came. I guess I thought we could really *do* something."
Ellen made a half-turn, taking in the command shack, the compound, the women who remained. "Isn't this enough?"
"I have to get on with my *life*."
Ellen said, "This is mine."

"Oh, Vic, I've been so stupid." June was sobbing in Vic's arms. She was also lying in her teeth but she didn't care, she was sick of the revolution and she was going to have to go through this formula before Vic would allow her to resume her place at his kitchen sink. The work was still boring and stupid but at least there was less of it than there had been at camp; her bed was softer, and since it was coming on winter, she was grateful for the storm sashes, which Vic put up every November, and the warmth of the oil burner, which he took apart and cleaned with his own hands every fall.

Sally found her house in good order, thanks to Zack, but there was several weeks' work piled up in her studio, and she had lost a couple of commissions. She opened her drawer to discover, with a smile, that Zack had washed at least one load of underwear with something red.

"I think we do better together," Zack said.

Sally said, "We always have."

In the wake of fraternization with the military guard detail, Marva discovered she was pregnant. She knew what Dr. Ora Fessenden said she was supposed to do, but she didn't think she wanted to.

As weeks passed, the women continued to drift away. "It's nice here and all," Betts said apologetically, "but there's a certain *je ne sais quoi* missing; I don't know what it is, but I'm going back down there and see if I can find it."

Glenda said, "Yeah, well. So long as there is a yang, I guess there is going to have to be a yin."

"Don't you mean, so long as there is a yin, there is going to have to be a yang?"

Glenda looked in the general direction of town, knowing there was nothing there for her to go back to. "I don't know what I mean any more."

Activity and numbers at the camp had decreased to the point where federal troops could be withdrawn. They were needed, as it turned out, to deal with wildcat raids in another part of the state. Those who had been on the scene came back with reports of incredible viciousness.

Standing at their windows in the town, the women could look up to the hills and see the campfire still burning, but as the months wore on, fewer and fewer of them looked and the column of smoke diminished in size because the remaining women were running out of volunteers whose turn it was to feed the fire.

Now that it was over, things went on more or less as they had before.

Pilots of the Purple Twilight

The wives spent every day by the pool at the Miramar, not far from the base, waiting for word about their men. The rents were cheap and nobody bothered them, which meant that no one came to patch the rotting stucco or kill centipedes for them or pull out the weeds growing up through the cracks in the cement. They were surrounded by lush undergrowth and bright flowers nobody knew the names for, and although they talked about going into town to shop or taking off for home, wherever that was, they needed to be together by the pool because this was where the men had left them and they seemed to need to keep claustrophobia as one of the conditions of their waiting.

On good days they revolved slowly in the sunlight, redolent of suntan oil and thorough in the exposure of all their surfaces because they wanted the tans to be *right* for the homecoming, but they also knew they had plenty of time. If it rained they would huddle under the fading canopy and play bridge and canasta and gin, keeping scores into the hundreds of thousands even though they were sick of cards. They did their nails and eyebrows and read Perry Mason paperbacks until they were bored to extinction, bitching and waiting for the mail. Everybody took jealous note of the letters received, which never matched the number of letters sent because mail was never forwarded after a man was reported missing. The women wrote anyway, and every day at ten they swarmed down the rutted drive to fall on the mailman like black widow spiders, ravenous. Most of the letters were for the wretches whose husbands had already come *home*, for God's sake, whisking them away to endlessly messy kitchens and perpetual heaps of laundry in dream houses mortgaged on the GI Bill. Embarrassed by joy, they had left the Miramar without a backward glance, and for the same reason they always wrote at least once, stuffing their letters with vapid-looking snapshots of first babies, posting them from suburbs on the other side of the world.

At suppertime they all went into the rambling stucco building, wrenching open the rusting casements because it seemed important to keep sight of the road. Just before the shadows merged to make darkness they would drift outside again, listening, because planes still flew out from the nearby base every morning and, waiting, they were fixed on the idea of counting them back in. Most of their men had left in ships or on foot but still they waited. To the women at the Miramar every dawn patrol hinted at a twilight return, and the distant Fokkers or P-38s or F-87s seemed appropriate emblems for their own hopes, the suspense a fitting shape to place on the tautening stomachs, the straining ears, the dread of the telegram.

They all knew what they would do when the men came back even though they had written their love scenes privately. There would be the reunion in the crowded station, the embrace that would shut out everybody else. She would be standing at the sink when he came up from behind and put his arms around her waist, or she would be darning or reading, not thinking about him just for once, when a door would open and she would hear him: Honey, I'm home. There would be the embrace at the end of the driveway, the embrace in plain view, the embrace in the field. None of them thought about what he would be like when they embraced, what he must look like now, the way he really smelled, because their memories had been stamped with images distilled, perfected by the quality of their own waiting, the balance they tried to keep between thinking about it and not thinking about it. *If I can just manage not to think about it*, Elise still told herself, *then maybe he will come*.

Watching the sky, even after all these years, she would be sure she heard the distant vibration of motors drumming, or maybe it was the jet sound, tearing the sky like a scythe; she had been there since Chateau Thierry, or was it Amiens, and she knew the exact moment at which it became too dark to hope. "Tomorrow," she would say, and because the others preferred to think she was the oldest and so was the best at waiting, they would follow her inside. They all secretly feared that there was an even older woman bedridden in the tower, and that her husband had sailed with Enoch Arden, but nobody wanted to know for sure. They preferred to look to Elise, who kept herself beautifully and was still smiling; she had survived.

They were soft at night, jellied with anticipation and memory, one in spirit with Elise, but each morning found them clattering out to the chaises with Pam and Marge, hard and bright. Pam and Marge were the leaders of a group of self-styled girls in their fifties, who had greying hair and thickening waists. They liked to kid and whistled songs like "Praise the Lord and Pass the Ammunition" through their teeth. They shared a home-front camaraderie that enraged Donna, who was younger, and who had sent her husband off to a war nobody much remembered. She and Sharon and a couple of others in their forties would press their temples with their fists, grumbling about grand-standing, and people who still thought fighting was to be admired. Anxious, bored, frazzled by waiting, these two groups indulged in a number of diverting games: who had the most mail and who was going to sit at the round table at supper, who was hogging all the sunlight. They chose to ignore the newcomers, mere slips of things who had sent their men off to—where was it— Nam, or someplace worse.

Pam and Marge were tugging back and forth with Donna and Sharon this particular morning, wrangling over who was going to sit next to Elise, when Peggy walked in. Her shoes were sandy from the walk up the long driveway and her brave going-away outfit was already rusty with sweat. Bill had put her in a cab for the Miramar because, as he pointed out, he wasn't going to be gone for long and she would be better off with other service wives, they would have so much in common.

"Bitch," Marge was saying, "look what you did to my magazines."

Donna dumped her makeup kit and portable radio on the chaise. "It serves you right."

Marge was red-faced and hot, she may not even have heard herself lashing out. "I hope it crashes."

Even Pam was shocked. "Marge!"

"It would serve her right."

Peggy dropped her overnight bag. "Stop it."

Donna had gone white. "Don't ever say that."

"Stop." Peggy set her fist against her teeth.

"Girls." Elise stood between them, frail and ladylike in voile. "What would Harry and Ralph think if they could see you now?"

Donna and Marge stood back, pink with shame.

"What is this new girl going to think?"

"I'm sorry," Marge said, and she and Donna hugged.

Elise saw that Peggy was backing away, ready to make a break for it. The perfect hostess, she put a hand on her arm. "Come and sit by me, ah . . ." She inclined her head graciously.

"Peggy."

"Come, Peggy." She patted the chaise. "I want you to meet Donna, her Ralph is in the Kula Gulf, and Pam and Marge both have husbands at, yes, that's it, Corregidor."

"But they couldn't."

Elise said, serenely, "Won't you have some iced tea?"

Peggy was gauging the distance between her and the overnight bag, looking for a gap in the overgrown greenery. "I can't stay."

"You'll have to excuse the girls," Elise said. "Everybody is a little taut, you understand."

"I don't belong here, I'm . . ."

Elise spoke gently, overlapping, ". . . only here for a little while. I know."

"Bill promised."

"Of course he did."

Later, when she felt better, Peggy let Elise lead her inside the cavernous building. She unpacked her things and after she had changed into her bikini she went out to take her place by the pool. She thought she would join the other girls in bikinis, who looked closer to her age, but they sat in closed ranks at the far end of the pool, giving her guarded looks of such hostility that she hurried back to her place by Elise.

"Don't mind them," Elise said. "It takes time to adjust."

Going down to dinner, Peggy understood how important it was to be well-groomed. The room was bright with printed playsuits and pretty shifts in floral patterns chosen in fits of bravery. Although there were only women in the room, each of them had taken care with her hair and makeup, pressing her outfit because it was important; if they flagged, the men might discover them and be disgusted, or else the word would get out that they had given up, and there was no telling what grief that would bring. Either way they would never be forgiven. Whether or not the men came they would face each dinner hour tanned and combed and carefully made up, and no matter what it cost, they would be smiling.

That night Pam and Marge were never better; they had on their sharkskin shorts with the bright jersey shirts knotted under their breasts to expose brown bellies, and when Betty joined them at the end of the dining room they went into their Andrews Sisters imitation with a verve that left everybody shouting. Jane played the intro again and again, and even though they were spent and gasping, they came tapdancing back. There was a mood of antic pleasure which had partly to do with the new girl in the audience, and partly with the possibility that the men just might come back and discover them at a high point: *See how well we do without you. Look how pretty we are, how lively. How could you bear to leave us for long?* They imagined the men laughing and hooting the way they did for USO shows; at the finale, the women would bring them up on stage.

Bernice was next with "I'll be seeing you," and they were all completely still by the time Donna took the microphone and sang, "Fly the Ocean in a Silver Plane." Then it was time to go outside.

"Tell me about him," Elise said, leading Peggy through the trees.

Peggy said, "He has blue eyes."

"Of course he does. Gailliard has blue eyes."

"Who?"

"Gailliard. He crushed my two hands in one of his, and when I cried out he said, Did I hurt you, and I had to let him think he had pinched my fingers because I didn't want to let him know I was afraid." She whispered. "I'm still afraid."

This old lady? Peggy wanted to support her. *Oh Lord.*

"Harry always kisses me very sweetly," Pam was saying to Marge, "he only opens his mouth a little."

Marge said, "Dave promised to bring me a dish carved out of Koa wood. Have you ever seen Koa wood?"

Donna and her group muttered together; they had been schooled to believe it was important not to let any of it show.

None of the young things seemed to know what they thought about the parting. Still they came out into the evening with all the others, straining as if they too were convinced of the return. Marva knew they didn't even speak the same language as the old ladies, who would talk about duty and patriotism and, what was it, the job that had to be done. She and Ben and a whole bunch of others had been together in the commune, like puppies, until they came for him because he had thrown away the piece of paper with the draft call, the MP kicked him and said, Son, you ought to be damn glad to go. Now here was this new girl not any older than Marva but her husband was what they called a career man, she probably believed in all that junk the old ladies believed in, so she could learn to play canasta and go to hell.

At first Peggy was afraid of the shadows; then the figures in the field sorted themselves out so that she could see which were trees and which were women running across the grass like little girls, stretching their arms upwards, and she found herself swallowing rage because this place was worse than any ghetto. The women were all either stringy and bitter or big-assed and foolish and Bill had dumped her here as if she were no better than the rest of them. When Elise tried to take her hand she pulled away.

"It's going to be all right."

"This is terrible."

"You'll get used to it."

"Listen." Marge's voice lifted. "Do you hear anything?"

Waiting, they all stood apart because each departure shimmered in the air at this moment of possible return.

Elise remembered that Gailliard had taken her to the balcony at the Officers' Club. He had set her up on the rail in her grey chiffon with the grey suede slippers and then he stood back to regard her, so handsome that she wanted to cry out, and she remembered that at the time they were so steeped in innocence that each departure of necessity spelled victory and swift return. She wondered if old ladies were supposed to feel the hunger that stirred her when she remembered his body. She wondered if he was still loyal, after all these years. In retrospect their love was so perfect that she knew he would always be beautiful, as she remembered him, and true.

Pam and Marge had said goodbye in peacetime; when Harry and Dave flew out from Pearl in April of that year it had seemed like just another departure. Marge could remember dancing with Dave's picture, relieved, in a way, because the picture never belched or scratched its belly, although she and Pam stoutly believed that if they had known there was going to be a war they could have surrounded the parting with the right number of tears and misgivings, enough prayers to prepare for the return. Their fears would have been camouflaged by bright grins because, when you were a service wife, you had to treat every parting like every other parting. Still . . .'

Bernice's husband Rob enlisted in the first flush of patriotism after Pearl Harbor. "Go," she said, clenching her fists to keep from grabbing him. He looked back once: "At least I'm doing the right thing." *He's off there accomplishing things with a bunch of other guys, they're busy all day and at night they relax and horse around while I am stuck here, getting older, with nothing to do except sing that song on Saturday nights . . .* Donna remembered her and Ralph on the bed, wondering what sense it made for him to go into the mess in Korea. There was no choice and so, laying resignation between them like a knife-blade, they made love one last time. Marva remembered being stoned in that commune near Camp Pendleton, Ben would come in looking like Donald Duck in that uniform and all the kids would laugh, but the last time he made her pick up her bedroll and he brought her here, he told her he would be back and maybe he would.

Peggy nursed a secret hurt: what Bill said to her in a rage right before he dumped her at the Miramar: "If you can't wait more than five minutes, why should I bother to come back," and her riposte: "Don't bother," so when Marge yelled, "I think I hear something," she had to run to the edge of the clearing with the rest of them; at the first sound they would light the flares. She heard herself calling aloud, thinking if anything happened to Bill it would be her fault, for willing it, and that if she spread her arms and cried, "They're coming," it might bring them.

She discovered that the days were exquisitely organized around their waiting; no one sunned or played cards or read for too long in any one day because it would distort the schedule; they had to keep the division between the segments because it made the hours keep marching. Although fights were a constant, no quarrel could be too violent to preclude a reconciliation because they had to continue together, even as they had to silence any suggestion that even one of them might be disappointed; when the men came back they were all coming, down to the last one. Unless this was so, there was no way for the women to live together.

Pam and Marge organized a softball team, mostly thick-waisted "girls" from their own age group. They got Peggy to play, and after some consideration Donna joined them.

"Wait till you meet Dave," Marge said, sprawling in the grass in the outfield. "I would see him at the end of the walk in his uniform and that was when I loved him most. He'll never change."

"Everybody changes," Donna said gently.

"Not my Dave."

"Now Bill . . ." Peggy began, but when she tried to think of Bill there was a blur and what she remembered was not what he looked like but what she wanted him to look like because she had always been bothered by the hair growing in his nostrils, his wide Mongol cheekbones, covered by too much flesh, so she recomposed his face to her liking: If I can't have what I had, then at least let me make it what I want. "Bill looks like something out of the movies."

Somebody decided it would be a good idea to have bonfires ready; if the planes should come by daylight they would see the smoke columns. Every few weeks the women could rebuild the heaps of firewood, taking out anything that looked wet or rotten. Bernice organized a duplicate bridge tournament. Marva and some of the younger girls meditated for half an hour before breakfast and again before supper and, grudgingly, asked Peggy to join them.

She and Peggy were the first at the chaises one bright morning and they exchanged stories, grumbling about being stuck with all these old biddies, no better off than anybody else.

"I don't know," Marva was saying, "at least the meals come regular. I got sick of granola."

Peggy said, "I never had a tan like this before."

"But they act like we're going to be here forever." Marva looked at Marge, wabbling out on wedgies. "It's obscene."

Peggy said, bravely, "We're not like them."

"We'll never be like them."

"We just have to hang in here for the time being." Peggy settled herself, feeling the sun on her belly. "For the time being we're in the same boat."

Elise seemed especially drawn to Peggy; she would pat the chaise next to her and wait for Peggy to join her. Then she would put the name, Gailliard, into the air between them and sit contemplating it, assuming that Peggy shared some of the same feelings. She told herself Peggy was young enough to be her daughter but that was a lie; she could be Peggy's grandmother, and knew it. Still it seemed important to her to keep the pretense of youth, even as it was important to keep herself exquisitely groomed and to greet each morning with the same generous smile, the same air of hope because to the others she was a fixed point, which they could sight from, and until she flagged they would not waver. She did her best to suspend Peggy in that same network of waiting, to keep her safe with the rest.

"You ought to talk to Donna," she said, "I think you have a lot in common."

"I'm afraid of her because she seems so sad."

"You could learn from her," Elise said. "She keeps herself well."

Peggy knew what Elise meant. Pam and Marge and their group played records over and over and mooned and dithered like a bunch of girls but Donna kept her dignity, fixed in a purity of waiting which Elise would admire because it resembled her own. There was no way for Peggy to explain that she and Bill had parted in anger, that she was pledged to wait but she had already jeopardized everything she was waiting for, that in her failure of will she might already have wished Bill to his death.

Please bring him back, she thought. *I would give anything to have him back.*

By the time she thought this she had already been there longer than she realized; time blurred, and as she sent out her wish she heard the distant drumming of engines and the sky darkened with planes returning, the message running ahead of them, singing in the air at the Miramar, hanging before them as clearly as anything in writing:

I'M BACK

so that Peggy had to hide her head and rock with anxiety and it was Donna who was the first to acknowledge it, addressing the sky gently, her voice soft with several lifetimes of regret.

She said, so nobody else heard her: "I'm afraid it's too late."

Elise found her hands fluttering about her face and her loins weak and her head buzzing in panic. Even with her eyes closed she was aware of Gailliard shimmering before her, beautiful and unscathed, and she pulled a towel up to cover her, murmuring, "He'll see me, he'll *see* me," because she knew that he would come to her with his beauty preserved at the moment when his life went out like a spark and she was well past seventy now, beautifully groomed but old, wrinkled, with all her systems crumbling, diminished even further by his relentless beauty, and if he recognized her at all he would say, You're so *old*. She pulled the towel closer, like a shroud, whispering. "Please don't let him see me."

HONEY, IT'S ME

(Donna murmured, "There's nothing left here.")

"You bastard, wasting me like this, while you stayed young." Bernice went to her room and pulled the curtains and slammed the door.

Marge was ablaze with love, and she sang, or prayed: Dave, let me keep you out there, perfect and unchanged. If you come you will have a beer belly, just like me, you will have gotten grey. As she sang, or prayed, she imagined she heard him responding: How could I, I've been dead, and she said, aloud, "Dave, let me keep you the way I thought you were."

DON'T YOU HEAR ME

(In the tower, the oldest lady turned milky eyes to the ceiling; she could no longer speak but she made herself understood: *It was all used up by waiting*.)

Peggy cowered; they were supposed to light the flares or something—set off fires. Remembering the story of the monkey's paw she thought her last wish had come true and that Bill was struggling out of some distant heap of wreckage at this very minute, and he would be mangled, dreadful, dragging toward her . . .

"The meals aren't bad," Marva was saying, doing her best to override the thunder of the engines; the sky above was black now, but she pushed on, "and Ben, he never really gave a damn." Shrugging as if to brush aside the shadows of the wings, she said, "Hey, Peg, do you hear anything?"

. . . either that or he would try and yank her away from this place that she loved just to go on making her unhappy. He would be Enoch Arden, at the window, and she would turn to face him: Oh, it's you.

"No," Peggy said firmly, as the planes passed over, "I don't hear anything."

The Thing at Wedgerley

When Vernon threw himself against the doors of the deserted mansion he knew more or less what he was getting into. The door knocker, under the plaque that said Wedgerley, was a face, and the mouth opened as he watched, emitting a warning scream.

Lightning flashes revealed brooding turrets and shattered windows, and on one of the flashes he was sure he saw something moving deep inside the house. Still he was saturated, his second-best tweed coat was beginning to shrink under the vicious rain; he was already shivering and he knew that with the car mired up to the axles and no lights showing along the road for miles, he was going to pass the night in this house.

He would have been just as dry and definitely safer in the stables, but generations of Gavers had slept in stables in the Old Country; Vernon Gaver had worked hard, he had even married a hideous, wealthy bitch to bring himself this far, and by George he was going to sleep in the big house, and he was going in by the front door.

When he rang and nobody came and he pounded and nobody came, he broke the frosted glass panel with one arm swathed in his raincoat and then fumbled until he found the latch. The door creaked with the rust of the ages and as he came into the hall he thought he heard, from far off, a deep and rusty laugh. He fumbled for the light switch and when no lights came on he broke a chair and wrapped one leg with part of a drapery to make a dusty torch.

The surprising thing was, when he broke the chair, he thought he heard it scream in pain, and the draperies ripped away with a sound like a woman's sigh. It took him several minutes to get the thing lighted; he had to empty his spare tin of lighter fluid on it and then he had to scratch his way through three damp packs of matches because his lighter wouldn't work.

Once he had it going, he looked around with growing misgivings. The place looked as if it hadn't been occupied in years. Dust covers made grim shapes out of all the furniture, and as he looked around he could swear he saw one of those shapes move.

He swallowed hard, only partially surprised by the sound of roaring in his ears. The cobwebs were disturbing, the shadows were disturbing, and the most disturbing thing of all was the tracks, not footprints exactly, but trailing tracks, as of something which had dragged itself across the dusty floor. They began not at the door but some distance down the hall and they ended in the middle of a room, as if whatever it was had levitated, picking up and setting down at will. He was only partially surprised when he discovered, on the prayer rug in one of the sitting rooms, a pool of fresh blood, and when he found the severed foot he only blanched and kicked it under a chair. Something, he thought, was trying to warn him. Something wanted to scare him away.

"You can't frighten me," he said, aloud, and then shrank at the sound of his voice echoing in all the dusty rooms and cast back at him by what seemed to be a chorus of voices, which went, E-e-e-e-e.

He couldn't help wishing he had his Newfoundland. He and Bounder would stalk through the halls without a trace of fear because nothing would dare brave Bounder's iron jaws, and when they were sleepy they would lie down together, he would make himself warm by nestling against Bounder's dense, woolly coat. But Bounder was locked in the basement storage room at home, along with the deep-freeze and all their winter clothes and the Exercycle, Myrna's revenge because he had spent the entire AT&T dividend check on a side of horsemeat for the dog, when she had wanted to spend it on a trip to Rio to have some of her flab excised.

Damn Myrna, he thought, and her mother and her sister too. All of them up there in the apartment, feeding on him. Well he had been their creature long enough. When he got home from this night, if he made it through the night, things were going to be different. He shrank at the sound of another thunder crack, and then he opened his mouth wide, as if it would help him hear better. He thought he heard something moving somewhere deep inside the house.

The library would be the best place, he thought, and he broke up a side table and a couple of chairs to make a fire, and uncovered the sofa, beating out the dust before he lay down to sleep. He hadn't realized he was so tired. He fell asleep with his cheek pressed against the hard edge of a flashlight he had found.

When he woke the fire had burned down and there was Something in the room.

Vernon felt the chill seize him; his teeth clamped shut and every hair on his body took on a life of its own but he forced back panic and managed to turn on the flashlight.

The Thing was almost upon him, and it was hideous. Rotting flesh fell away from the skull and hung from its arms like cerements, almost one with the tattered, mouldy garment which covered it. Its fangs were bared and its talons raised. Its voice came as from a deep void.

"I'm going to get you," It said.

Vernon halted It with his flashlight. "Listen," he said, "I came to get *you*."

"*Get* you," It said. "I'm hungry, and I need to feed."

"No kidding I'm here to make a deal." As the Thing faltered Vernon added, hastily, "There's plenty in it for you."

"What do you mean, plenty?"

"Plump flesh, fresh blood. But you have to do something for me."

Despite Itself, the Thing began to slaver. "What do you want?"

"I want you to get rid of my wife."

"And what do I get?"

"You get her, she weighs two-fifty in the buff." As Vernon watched, saliva threaded itself between the hideous, gaping jaws. "And I'll tell you what," he added. "I'll throw in her mother and sister too."

What passed for the Thing's eyes glowed phosphorescent in empty sockets. Vernon could swear he could see right through to the back of Its skull. "When do I start?"

"Well, there's a hitch," Vernon said. "I can't bring them here, I can't get them to do anything. You'll have to come to them. You don't evaporate in sunlight or anything like that, do you?"

The Thing drew Itself up. "You forget who you're talking to," It said with pride. "I'm the Wedgerley Thing."

Vernon and the Thing set forth as soon as it got light; the Thing lifted Vernon's car by its front axle and pulled it out of the mud.

"Hey," Vernon said. "That's really terrific."

"I keep in shape." The Thing preened. "When you're a living legend and all, you have to take care of yourself. How many people do you think I've eaten? Guess."

"A hundred," Vernon said.

"Hardly a drop in the bucket," said the Thing. "What I do when I catch them is, first I drink out all their blood, and then . . ."

He gave It a considered look. "Listen, since we have to go into town and all?"

The phosphorescence was overshadowed by the sunlight but Vernon thought It was looking in his direction. "Yes?"

"Maybe you'd better put on this raincoat. And how about wearing my hat?"

On the way back to his apartment, he had the uncomfortable feeling he was talking to a rack of bones, something that had died in the car, and partly for his own sake, he kept up a constant chatter to entertain It. He told It how he had met Myrna and married her for a place in her father's business, how the father had died broke and how Myrna and her mother and her sister had been crammed into the one apartment like three fat leeches ever since. He told It how Bounder was his only friend, the only thing that loved him, and he thought he detected a faint flicker of interest, a twitch of the naked finger bones, so he went on at length about the dog, what he ate, how he was going to let him out of the cellar and the two of them were going to have wonderful times together once the women were gone. In a fit of camaraderie, he promised the Thing one of Bounder's horsemeat steaks. Between himself, he managed to fill the silence until they pulled up in the parking lot outside Vernon's building and the Thing finally spoke.

"You didn't tell me you lived in a high-rise."

"I thought you were supposed to be able to levitate."

"To the twenty-eighth *floor*?"

"All right," Vernon said with a sigh, and he took the Thing in by the basement door, past the storage lockers where they said a brief hello to Bounder, and on to the service elevator.

"This is it," he said, opening the apartment door for

the Thing. "Honey," he yoo-hooed. "I'm *home.*" Then he slammed the door behind the Thing and leaned against it until he heard the women start to scream. After that he went to the movies, a double feature. If he stayed away long enough the messy part would be over with and the Thing might even get Itself back to Wedgerley, without him having to give It a ride.

When he got back it was almost dark. The apartment was empty and there was no signs of violence. He went through all the rooms calling; first he called Myrna and the other women, and then, for form's sake, he called the Thing. He decided, finally, that once It was sated, It must have just dematerialized.

Just as well, he thought. It wouldn't be around expecting his friendship, making demands. He had never really been comfortable with It. Those claws were hideous, and those fangs . . .

Once he had satisfied himself that they were gone and It was gone, he went to the basement to get Bounder. "Come on, Bounder, baby, come on boy," he sang out as he approached their storage room. "Nobody's going to kick you off the bed tonight."

As he unlocked the door, somebody laughed. The door slammed shut behind him as he stepped inside.

The Thing hadn't gone home after all. It had on Vernon's best tweed jacket and Vernon's favorite slippers and It was crouched on top of the deepfreeze, whose contents included twenty frozen chickens and the side of horsemeat as well as the leg of lamb It was gnawing, and lying next to the freezer was Bounder's fluffy corpse. He couldn't see Myrna or the others, but he could hear them laughing.

"What happened?"

"They made me a better offer," the Thing said, and lunged for Vernon's throat.

Gran

In the evenings Gran would sit in her rocker on the front porch and look dead. She was approaching her hundredth birthday, her eyes were pits and her skin stretched tight over her elegant skull, so that when she sat forward in her rocker with both hands steadying her, cane between her knees and her chin propped on her hands, she had a detached, monumental look which frightened passers-by.

A little drink every night before supper, Gran told the reporter who came to write up her hundredth birthday. A little drink and one cigar a day, she said, but nobody understood her any more except for Cousin Thrall, who leaned close and then said to the reporter:—

"A good clean life. That's what keeps her looking so young." Gran wasn't able to eat the cake because it would be bad for her and so the reporter and the photographer shared it with the family: Steve, Edna and the kids, who were so used to having their great-grandmother in the house that they treated her like another piece of furniture; except for Cousin Thrall, whose task it was to take care of Gran. Gran had all the money, it was still in her name, but she had remembered the family generously in her will, and, in their own way, they were proud of her.

"She remembers when everybody went places on foot."

It's all different now, Gran told the reporter. People ain't strong like they used to be. People have changed.

Sid and Polly, the kids, elbowed each other resentfully, but neither of them said anything. Gran liked to put a bony hand on them when they weren't looking, and when they jumped and squealed she would shout into their ear, "Soft, that's what you are. Soft." Nobody respects old people the way they used to, Gran was saying.

The reporter said, "What?"

Cousin Thrall said, "She says people have got away from nature, she wants to get back to the earth, like it was in the old days."

Steve said, to make a better story, "We've promised Gran to take her camping in Canada this summer. Revisit scenes of her youth."

The reporter said, "That's wonderful." He leaned forward to catch what Gran was mumbling. "What?"

Gran yelled, *You be sure and put that in the paper*. She had to yell; she was so deaf she was afraid he wouldn't hear.

Cousin Thrall said, "She once played the harp for Thomas Edison. He listened to her on the telephone."

Of course once the thing about the trip appeared in the paper, the family had to go through with it; if they didn't, they would look fools.

"Who knows," Edna said to Steve, "maybe the excitement will carry her off." Then she began to cry because she was ashamed, it was just that she and Steve and the kids never had a minute alone.

"Don't feel bad, honey," Steve said, "she always says she's tired of living. We'll give her a real send-off."

"Well," Edna said, to make herself feel better, "she deserves to see the homestead one last time."

Edna knew perfectly well with those cataracts Gran couldn't see anything, but Steve didn't remind her.

So they went. Gran picked out her clothes for the trip: the lavender dress with the lace fichu, the black stockings and orthopedic oxfords with tassels on the ties, her cameo, her Persian lamb cape even though it was summer, her black straw hat. Then Steve and Edna and the kids and Cousin Thrall all piled in the stationwagon with their luggage in the tent trailer and the aluminum rowboat lashed to the top and Gran propped between Steve and Edna in the front.

Gran retreated from them, so that when they did stop somewhere in Canada, they had to shake her and shake her to rouse her. She took a little tea and then fell into a deep dream; she was sitting in the field amid trees and flowers and without warning a great chasm opened in front of her. She contemplated the chasm until morning and left it regretfully because Cousin Thrall was standing over her saying it was time to get up and hit the road.

The second day she began to smell the trees, and in the recesses of her mind her young self began to uncurl and flex, until it bumped into her memories.

Gran remembered the mornings in Canada, intolerably cold; she remembered laboring for Old Sam, her husband, who mistreated her in bed and in town alike; she remembered the pain of giving birth and the deeper pain when her children got big enough to be embarrassed by her plain ways; compared to that, the past few years with Sam and Edna had been like a dream but her eyes were gone now, she could no longer mend or crochet and so she was of no use to them; she knew it was time to go, but her body wasn't ready.

"So here we are, Gran. Gran?"

"Gran, Gran! My God, Edna, I think she may be dead."

"She's only sleeping."

"I don't think so. She won't breathe on this mirror. She's died, Edna."

"Poor old thing."

None of them could know it, but Gran was still locked inside there somewhere, but now her jaw was fixed and nothing else would work. She thought to rouse herself, to sniff the air, to pull up her skirts and blunder into the field, but when she sent messages to her muscles they froze, so that finally nothing moved.

Polly was crying. "She's dead. Oh Mommy, she's sitting right there and she's *dead*."

Steve tried to comfort her. "Don't worry, honey, it's just Gran."

"But it's different. She's a dead person now."

Somewhere deep inside, the spark of Gran listened as from a great distance.

Edna said, gently, "Let's take her home."

"It's not that easy," Steve said. "She died on foreign soil."

"I don't see what difference that makes."

"Papers. Certificates at the border."

"Why can't we just tell them we're taking her home?"

"You don't understand," said Steve, who was a lawyer. "It could tie up the will for years. She has to 'die' after we get home."

"If she sits where she is they'll never notice."

"Oh, Mommy," Polly's voice rose to a wail. "She can't ride in here with *us*."

Finally they decided to put her on top. She was already fixed in a sitting position so they laid her on her side on a cushion of blankets under the overturned aluminum rowboat, and they lashed the whole arrangement to the top of the car.

"She was really so sweet," Edna said.

Steve patted the rowboat. "Goodnight, Gran."

Edna said, as if nothing had happened, "Just think, Thrall, you can have Gran's room."

Then they crossed their fingers and headed for the border. As it turned out, there wasn't the slightest cause to worry. The inspector peeked under the tarp on the tent trailer and riffled through one suitcase as a matter of routine and then rapped his knuckles smartly on the boat and let them through. They were all so pleased and relieved that they pulled into the very next Howard Johnson's to celebrate; they were busy singing *Row Row Row Your Boat* in rounds, even Cousin Thrall, and so they went right past the sharp-nosed boy and the frowsy girl lurking in the parking lot; everybody had fried clams and orange freezes without a second thought for the car.

When they came out the car was gone.

"Don't worry," Steve said, without thinking about it, "I'll notify the police and they won't get far."

"Oh, Lord," Edna said, biting down hard on her knuckles. "Gran."

Gran was under the rowboat when they took the car, but how could Tommy and Cheryl know? She was still alive, too, but since they didn't even know she was there, they couldn't know that either, and even if she had been there on the seat between them, there was nothing left to prove there was any life in there except for a tiny pulse throbbing under her silvery hair. She was in a dream of her girlhood, lying in the grass with a boy she had loved once, who had been killed in the war; as soon as she was freed from her body she would go and look for him and they would be together forever, two puffs of vapor radiantly entwined.

When they got far enough away from the Howard Johnson's, Tommy stopped the wagon and unhooked the tent trailer. Then he and Cheryl set it on fire and stood with their arms round each other as it crashed, flaming, into a gorge. Then they got back in the car and kissed each other hard.

"This is a good car," he said to Cheryl. "It's going to take us a long way."

"All the way to California."

"I can lie on my back in an orange grove."

"Some day they're going to put me in the movies. They can find me working in a topless bar."

"This bus has got a lot of room," Tommy said, "it'll hold all the money we can heist and then some more."

"It's clean," Cheryl said, patting the front seat fondly. "We didn't have to get blood on it, like with the Buick."

"Man, remember how that guy prayed and cried."

"I never liked the Buick, anyway."

"Listen, didn't we mow down that trooper and never feel a bump?"

"Mowed him down like nothing."

"Yeah, man," Tommy said, with a reminiscent sigh. He turned on the motor and they scratched off.

Under the rowboat, Gran had begun drifting through layers of pearlescent clouds, beginning a long passage; she could feel the gradual but steady lifting of pressure from her soul as the car bore her along, stiffened and serene.

She was almost called back once, by a spatter of shots and a scream that took a long time to stop, but after a while everything was quiet again and she felt, dimly, the sensation of continuing motion, so that she was able to continue her progress uninterrupted.

Inside the car, Cheryl was crying and Tommy had to sock her to make her stop.

"I'm sorry, Tommy."

"Then shut up."

"I can't help it."

He hugged her. "I'm sorry I hit you, all right?"

"That ain't it." Her lower lip was still fluttering.

"It's what you did to that lady . . ."

"You saw, I had to do it."

". . . I just looked at her and well—it could have been me."

"The hell it could, honey." Tommy felt good.

Cheryl was still crying.

They were way West now, the trees were thinning out and after a while there would be no more water. Tommy saw a glint through the trees ahead. "Hey, looky, there's some kind of lake or something. Great, huh?"

"No." Cheryl was sniffling. "Look, it got on my dress."

"Tell you what," he said, to make her feel better, "We'll go skinny-dipping and you can wash it out."

"I don't know."

"And afterwards," he said, pleased with the thought, "afterwards I'll take you out in that goddam boat."

By the time they reached the reservoir, Cheryl was humming, because she felt better. She tied up her hair so it wouldn't get wet and then she made Tommy turn his back while she went behind the car and took off her clothes. After a lot of thought she put back on her slip.

"Chicken," Tommy said, and stripped and went into the water like a knife.

Fragments of water lifted by their hands sparkled in the sun, and the blue sky spread above them, cloudless, unsullied by anything they might have done. Their white bodies were agile and beautiful and if Gran could have seen them she would have thought: God bless the young.

After Cheryl's dress dried they got their clothes on and Tommy went to get down the boat. He unlashed it and lifted it off like the carapace of a bug and there was Gran.

His voice went funny. "Cheryl! Cheryl, come here."

She was frightened, hushed. "Is she . . ."

"She's dead."

Cheryl said, "It gives me the creeps to think about it.

Us riding along like that, just as happy as the day is long and all the time . . ."

"All the time there she was up there."

"There she was," Cheryl concluded solemnly. "Dead."

"Son of a bitch."

There was a silence.

Tommy pulled himself together. "We got to get rid of her, or else they'll blame us."

Cheryl was getting shrill. "What are we going to *do*?"

"Cool it," Tommy said, replacing the boat. "I got an idea. Get in."

"With *her* up there?"

"I know it's spooky, but we have to."

"I can't help it," Cheryl said as they hurtled along. "It just gives me the *creeps*."

"We'll get rid of her in the desert," Tommy said. "Nobody will suspect."

When they reached a likely spot in the desert Tommy looked both ways to make sure there was no place anybody could watch them from and then he stopped the car and got out and got Gran down from underneath the boat. Then they arranged her carefully, brushing back her fine hair with due deference for the dead and fastening her cape and resettling her hat, and they left her sitting on a rock, looking out across the desert with bright, blind eyes.

After a while an Indian came along, and he found Gran sitting on the rock. She had drifted away some time between the day Tommy and Cheryl left her and the Indian found her, the sun had dried her and the sand tanned her and the Indian put a reverent hand on her fichu, thinking that the flowered straw hat and the Persian lamb cape were greatly to be admired.

He said a prayer to her and picked her up, holding her so that she faced over his shoulder, scanning the desert at his back with an unremitting stare.

After two days and nights, during which he stopped only to eat from his pack and take water, he reached a certain cave in the side of a mountain, where he set Gran down in a niche which looked as if it had been fashioned for her centuries before. After re-setting her hat and smoothing the Persian lamb cape, he bowed his head and left her, but he and his friends would come to visit her often, whether to worship her or only to admire, no one could be sure.

Tommy and Cheryl got theirs in a shoot-out in Slab City, which was no better than they deserved.

Unfortunately, with no legal proof of death, the Cunninghams were unable to settle the will, but for years afterwards they were able to sit around the television in the evenings and talk about what might have happened to Gran.

Death of a Monster

It would be safe to say the villagers didn't understand him. Even when he tried to make friends it went wrong. He was born not of woman but out of the laboratory, so naturally they hated him. He was too big, hideous, and when they heard what he had done (or what they thought he had done), they came boiling out into the streets with pikestaffs and torches, chasing him over the rooftops of that corny little village the way the Londoners chased Bill Sykes; he was not the last monster to run, gasping, into the desperate night. In the end he would accomplish his own destruction, toppling, again and again, into the fiery pit at the bottom of the laboratory, dragging the doctor's apparatus with him, but always leaving behind one or two retorts and a few of the good doctor's charred notes, so that he could be rediscovered, against his will, and reborn . . .

He would have a stake driven through his heart at the crossroads, in the middle of some perilous night.

Shrinking from the brandished crucifix, he would be caught outside his coffin as the sun came up; his face would contort with fear at the first shaft of holy light. It served him right, because he wanted more than anything to make others be like him. It wasn't their blood he was interested in, it was their souls.

Furry, regretful, he had no such designs; he just couldn't control himself once the moon changed him. Although they professed to feel sorry for him, they hated those funny tufts of fur between his fingers, those jaws. They weren't really afraid of him but they had to hunt him down anyway, because the monsters that would follow were too big and too remote to chase through darkened city streets. The giant tarantulas and pterodactyls to come would be too big to be kept at bay by crowds with torches; they would be too big even for army divisions or atomic weapons. The monsters to come would decimate entire battalions while the villagers sat home and wished they would go away, which they would do, eventually, like all those things from other planets and diseases from outer space, vanquished not by human powers but by inner corruption, proving too big or too horrendous to endure in our atmosphere.

Bubbling with pain, the creature sank back into the black lagoon as Grendel had centuries before, dying, but confident that it was by no means the last.

Ellen Warwick, who had tangled briefly with a junkie from Minneapolis, ran away to the woods two days before the pains started. Even before the twins were born she was overtaken by a great foreboding, an unspeakable message from tangled chromosomes; when she sat up to look at her babies she shrank in horror, although she could not have said at the time which of them was the monster because times were changing, and monsters are created by the times.

She named the twins Argul and Morgul. The ugly one

was Morgul; even new as he was, he was hideous, with his back already irremediably twisted and his head and body covered with warts. His mouth was huge and loose and she threw her poncho over him so she wouldn't have to see the rest. Beautiful as he was, Argul frightened her too. His brow was clear and his baby face flawless; the pupils of his eyes were already ringed with irises of a pale, relentless blue. He lay with his hands curved across his bosom like a tiny angel, so perfect that she had to turn away.

Her first instinct was to dispatch both of them, burying them in a single grave, but she knew she could not because they were, respectively, so ugly and so beautiful, and she did not know which she was supposed to fear. She was, after all, a mother. After some thought she wrapped them both in the poncho, leaving them in a little nest of leaves under a tree. Then, although she was weak and still bleeding, she found her way out of the woods and hitchhiked back to town.

The she-bear ambled into the clearing not long after Ellen had left it, perhaps attracted by the smell of blood, perhaps drawn by the babies' cries. Possessing no human standards for judging beauty, the she-bear did not have to decide between the little creatures, but only whether to eat them or mother them. She nosed at the poncho and sniffed them all over, and then licked them up and down thoughtfully, both Argul and Morgul, without regard for fair white skin or hideous warts, and, because she had just lost her own cubs, she took them as her own. When they got bigger she taught them how to find honey and hunt meat and so for a while they ran among the animals, happier than they would ever be again.

They might have been happy forever after if they had stayed with the she-bear, but her company did not suffice for long. At four, Argul was already dissatisfied, determined to walk erect even though none of the animals did and his own brother preferred to scuttle, hitching along on his knuckles. For no apparent reason, Argul made an arrangement of leaves and vines and tied it around his waist. When his brother saw and tried to brain him he went to the she-bear for solace. Rumbling low in her throat, she swatted him. He was gone within the week. She would mourn him for a few seasons, and then forget.

Morgul left that part of the forest with the bear's clawmarks across his mottled cheek. With Argul gone, he had taken up a club and pounded on his bear-mother's toes, feeding on her rage until she knocked him down.

Innately sad, driven by indefinable longings, Argul made his way out of the woods, coming to the fringes of the forest at last, dazzled by the sunlight on a field. He wandered for some hours, going down rows of unfamiliar plants, lying down at last at the intersection of two lines of stone so artfully laid together that he sensed the hand of a higher being. He woke in awe. Given a vocabulary, he would have thought: *angel*. Someone stood erect, his body covered, addressing Argul in a series of sounds which must have meaning.

"Od dam, yer a cute little bugger."

"Muh-muh-muh."

The farmer picked him up.

Argul had come home.

Morgul would be brought up by a blind forest ranger and his idiot son, who worked in partnership. The ranger took care of the boy, who, in turn, ran around and around the deck of the ranger's tower with his nose in the air, prepared to cry out at the first sign of smoke. So far there had been no fires to test either of them, and it was a perfect arrangement. In the evening the idiot boy sat at his father's feet, listening to an endless story which the old man had been stringing out night after night for years.

As it turned out, Morgul had to find them. Drawn by the sound of the old ranger's voice, Morgul broke through the undergrowth and discovered the watch tower, climbing hand over hand to reach the source of the sounds. At his father's knee, the idiot twisted restlessly, and in time began to whimper, grasping his father's wrist as Morgul appeared in the door.

"What is it, Arthur?"

"Hm-hm-hm . . ."

"Is it a fire?"

"N-n-n-n . . ."

The old man turned blind eyes towards the doorway. "Who is it?"

"Ha-ha-ha," Morgul said, and scuttled into the room.

"Why, it's a child."

The blind old man had no way of knowing how hideous Morgul was, and his idiot son Arthur had no way to tell him, so he took the repulsive little creature into his house and his bosom, teaching Morgul to talk and dress himself and take his turn watching for fires. The old man had a complete set of Milton and he troubled himself for some months, trying to think of some way to teach Morgul to read. Failing that, he broke off the endless story he had been telling Arthur and over the years he spun out instead the plots of the *Iliad* and the *Odyssey*, the Old Testament and the works of Alexandre Dumas, because it was his delight to teach and at last he had someone who could learn. He grew very fond of Morgul but he may have suspected the truth about him because he made him hide every time the state truck came to the tower to take away garbage or to bring supplies. The old man named him Richard, and mourned the fact that Arthur and Richard did not get along.

The farmer found Argul so beautiful that he named him Lance, although his own children had names like Brother and Willie and Lula Mae. Argul sat at his right hand at the long harvest table, bowing his head for the Bible reading at the beginning of the meal and again for the concluding grace. He worked willingly, and when he was old enough, went with the others to the country school, where the teachers had to work into the night devising new work for him to master. He was given a full scholarship to the state university at sixteen, but by that time Brother and Willie were in the service and Pa Gudger needed him to help work the farm. He grew in looks and virtue, apparently unaware of the stir he created among the girls.

Separated as they were, each with only dim memories of the other, the brothers shared a common dream, a ritual night of horror which engulfed the consciousness, whirling at a relentless pace until the dreamer's heart stopped for a moment and he woke to a dark room filled with his own screams.

At the farm Lula Mae often heard and came to comfort Argul, sitting on the edge of his bed in his sacking gown and holding his shoulders until he fell silent; he would touch her hand in thanks and they would part for the night, loving and chaste.

Morgul always woke to find the idiot hovering above him, gibbering in shared terror; He would cuff Arthur and then the two of them would huddle and whimper in opposite corners until it got light.

In the dream, he might be suffused with electricity, disintegrating, atom by atom, into a dizzying pain, or he would be strangling on his own tongue, shrinking from the blows of the sledgehammer as it pounded the stake through his heart, but most often he would be running over jagged stones or scrambling over rooftops, with the blood coursing into his eyes and more blood mixing with saliva, spinning out behind him in a lacy trail. There would be shouts and footsteps pounding behind him, rocks and brickbats getting closer to the mark, vicious whizzing knives, and his heart would fill his chest and throat, crowding against his teeth so there was no way he could turn and face them to shout: "Wait, I'm not who you think." Broken and aching from blows, he would run on and on, with all his clothes and some of the flesh flying in ribbons from his bleeding back, his bare feet cut by stones and his breath failing so that it was only a matter of time before they brought him to earth, overwhelming him with their hatred and crowing over his inevitable death.

Argul was convinced that it was a message from heaven and so tried to curb the evil side of his nature, if there was any evil in his nature.

Morgul knew it was a message from hell.

As he had as a child, Argul left home first. He had to make his fortune so he could marry Lula Mae and move to a farm of his own. He was nineteen, tall and fair, well versed in all the classics, especially the Bible, and he knew precisely what he wanted: to come back to the farm, marry, and live in peace and order for the rest of his life.

Lula Mae clung to him at the last minute. "Lance, don't go."

"I'll be back, honey. I have to earn enough money for us *and* Pa."

"Why can't we go on the way we are?"

"I don't know why," Argul said, "but I know that never works."

"Oh Lance," she said, and turned and ran into the house so he wouldn't see her cry.

On the forest ranger's tower, Morgul grew more and more restless; his head spun and his groin itched and he knew there had to be more to life than trees and the old man's boring books. He was sitting as he had sat for so many nights, listening to one more recital of *The Iliad*, when the idiot began to sniffle, rubbing his head against his father's knee.

"And then Hector came down . . . Oh, Arthur, what's the matter?"

The idiot was still crying. The word he said sounded like "Story," but he pointed at Morgul as he spoke.

"Oh yes, your story. I'm sorry, Arthur, I have neglected you."

The old man turned to Morgul, facing him over Arthur's head. "Did you hear that, Richard? He spoke. Say it again, Arthur, and I'll tell you the story."

This time it was clearer. "Sto-ry," Arthur said, but he was looking directly at Morgul and he might have meant, "Monster."

The old man took up the endless story just where he had left off the night Morgul first came to them, saying, "and then Arthur and his Daddy got up and had their breakfast, they had cereal and toast and milk, with sugar and milk on the cereal with a little bit of cinnamon, and then . . ."

Hours later Morgul got up, stultified, and went out on the deck. His groin was itching and he had to think. He could not stand another minute of that story, and the old man went on as if he would never stop. He didn't like Arthur's expression, either; Arthur had spoken, sooner or later he would give Morgul away to the old man, or worse, the authorities; it was only a matter of time. Inside, the old man said, "That's enough for tonight." He kissed Arthur and went to bed. Arthur came outside, snuffling; in another minute he would start running around and around the tower, on his nightly rounds. Morgul pounced and threw him off the deck. Then, with his blood high, he gave a great shout and left the tower forever, slouching towards a world which in other times might have received the message: DANGER, DANGER, vibrating with the warning as the monster approached.

On his first night in the city, he pounced on an old lady as she got out of a taxicab and had his way with her; he was astounded when she cried out for more. His next mark was a beautiful woman who took him home with her and introduced him to her husband, who was delighted to see him for a number of reasons, and who turned out to be keeping a pair of twelve-year-old boys and an Alsatian on the side. He was, however, appalled by Morgul's looks, and, whether prompted by aesthetics or a lingering jealousy of his wife, he offered Morgul orthopedic surgery and cosmetic corrections, saying, "After all, man, you don't *have* to go around looking like that."

"I like it." Morgul killed him and left. He was used to running along on his knuckles, he seemed to be fantastically successful with women and preferred looking like that; he was not, after all, a monster, because the first salient fact about a monster is that he cannot help what he is.

As it turned out, Argul had come to the same city, and at first he was wined and dined and feted because of his great good looks, but when woman after woman discovered that he would not come to her bed the people began to grumble against him, even though he was as polite as possible, explaining that he was being faithful to Lula Mae. What was worse, he would not lie even to please them, and he made himself unpopular by pointing out inconsistencies in people's life stories, uncovering petty and large embezzlements, infidelities and major thefts. He lost position after position because of a certain unwanted persistence of virtue, but he might have survived after all if he hadn't made the final mistake. It was the night he walked out on the orgy, pausing at the door to explain and so making the mistake which caused them all to turn on him and boil, howling, into the streets.

And so Argul was running along after all, as he and his twin had run in all those nightmares, and it was he who was the monster, pursued by villagers with murderous weapons and throats swelling with cries of rage and fear.

For a while it looked as if he might escape but he was caught in the middle of a flying leap by a hurtling brick and he fell into a crevice between two buildings, broken and already dying. Morgul, who was late for a necrophiliac brunch, happened to be passing through that same crevice, or alley, and so it happened that he reached Argul first.

They recognized each other on sight, saying:

"You."

The throngs from the orgy had been joined by outraged shopkeepers and vicious children; they were swarming down upon their monster, shrill in their pursuit.

Morgul peered into his brother's handsome, bloodied face. "What happened?"

Run to earth and dying, Argul shook his fair head, perplexed. "All I did was mention Sodom and Gomorrah. Oh yes," he said, in a dawning realization. "I told him I thought what they were doing might be wrong."

The crowd would be on them in another minute. Morgul knew there were certain associations he could not afford, and so when the crowd reached them he hit his brother with a rock. Then he scuttled off, juggling a mixture of feelings which would not trouble him for long. As it turned out, it was his rock that finished Argul, so Morgul was something of a hero. He acquired a rich patron who got him a job as a bouncer in a discotheque, and prospered to the end of his natural life.

Cynosure

"Now Polly Ann, Mrs. Brainerd might not like children, so I want you to go into the bedroom with Puff and Ambrose till we find out."

Polly Ann pulled her ruffles down over her ten-year-old paunch and picked up the cat, sausage curls bobbing as she went. "Yes Mama." She closed the bedroom door behind her and opened it again with a juicy, preadolescent giggle. "Ambrose made a puddle on the rug."

The three-note door chime sounded: Bong BONG Bong.

Norma motioned frantically. "Never *mind*."

"All *ri*-ight." The door closed on Polly Ann.

Then, giving her aqua faille pouf pillows a pat and running her hand over the limed oak television set, Norma Thayer, housewife, went to answer the door.

She had been working at being a housewife for years. She cleaned and cooked and went to PTA and bought every single new appliance advertised and just now she was a little sensitive about the whole thing because clean as she would, her husband had just left her, when there wasn't even an Other Woman to take the blame. Norma would have to be extra careful about herself from now on, being divorced as she was—especially now, when she and Polly Ann were getting started in a new neighborhood. They had a good start, really, because their new house in the development looked almost exactly like all the others in the block, except for being pink, and her furniture was the same shape and style as all the other furniture in all the other living rooms, right down to the formica dinette set visible in the dining area; she knew because she had gone around in the dark one night, and looked. But at the same time, she and Polly Ann didn't have a Daddy to come home at five o-clock, like the other houses did, and even though she and Polly Ann marked their house with wrought-iron numbers and put their garbage out in pastel plastic cans, even though they had centred their best lamp in the picture window and the kitchen was every bit as cute as the brochure said it was, the lack of a Daddy to put out the garbage and pot around in the yard on Saturdays and Sundays, just like everybody else, had put Norma at a distinct disadvantage.

Norma knew, just as well as anybody on the block, that a house was still a house without a Daddy, and things might even run smoother in the long run without all those cigarette butts and dirty pajamas to pick up, but she was something of a pioneer, because she was the first in the neighborhood to actually prove it out.

Now her next door neighbor was paying her first visit and Norma's housewifely heart began to swell. If all went well, Mrs. Brainerd would look at the sectional couch and the rug of salt-and-pepper cotton tweed (backed with rubber foam) and see that Daddy or no, Norma was just as good as any of the housewives in the magazines, and that her dishtowels were just as clean as any in the neighborhood. Then Mrs. Brainerd would offer her a recipe and invite her to the next day's morning coffee hour which, if she recollected properly, would be held at Mrs. Dowdy's, the lime split-level in the next block.

Patting the front of her Swirl housedress, she opened the door.

"Hello, Mrs. Brainerd."

"Hello," Mrs. Brainerd said. "Call me Clarice." She rubbed her hand along the lintel. "Woodwork looks real nice."

"Xerox," Norma said with a proud little smile, and let her in.

"Brassit on the doorknob," Mrs. Brainerd said.

"Works like a dream. I made some coffee," Norma said. "And a cake . . ."

"Never touch cake," Mrs. Brainerd said.

"No greasy feel . . ."

"Metrecookies," Mrs. Brainerd said, and her jaw was white and firm. "And no sugar for me. Sucaryl."

"If you'll just sit down here." Norma patted the contour chair.

"Thanks, no." Mrs. Brainerd smoothed *her* Swirl housedress and followed Norma into the kitchen.

She was small, slender, lipsticked and perfumed, and she was made of steel. Norma noticed with a guilty pang that Mrs. Brainerd fastened the neck of *her* housedress with a Sweetheart pin.

"Something special," Mrs. Brainerd said, noticing her looking at it. "Got it with labels from the Right Kind of Margarine." She brushed past Norma, not even looking at the darling little dining area. "Hm. Stains even bleach can't reach," she went on, peering into the sink.

Norma flushed. "I know. I scrubbed and scrubbed. I even used straight liquid bleach." She hung her head.

"Well." Clarice Brainerd reached into the pocket of her flowered skirt and came up with a shaker can. "Here," she said. She said it with a beautiful smile.

Norma recognized the brand. "Oh," she said, almost weeping with gratitude.

Clarice Brainerd had already turned to go. "And the can is decorated, so you'd be proud to have it in your living room."

"I know," Norma said, deeply moved. "I'll get two."

Her neighbor was at the back door now. Norma reached out, supplicating. "You're not leaving are you, before you even taste my cake . . ."

"You just try that cleanser," Clarice said. "And I'll be back."

"The morning coffee. I thought you might want me to come to the . . ."

"Maybe next time," her neighbor said, trying to be kind. "You know, you might have to entertain them here one day, and . . ." She looked significantly at the sink. "Just use that," she said reassuringly. "And I'll be back."

"I will." Norma bit her lip, torn between hope and despair. "Oh, I will."

"Cake," said Polly Ann just as the back door closed on Mrs. Brainerd's mechanically articulated smile. She came into the kitchen with Puff, the kitten, and Ambrose, the beagle, trailing dust and hairs behind. "I think Ambrose might be sick." She got herself some grape juice, spilling as she poured. A purple stain began to spread on the sink.

Norma reached out with the cleanser, wanting desperately to ward off the stain.

"He just did it again in the living room," Polly Ann said.

Norma's breath was wrenched from her in a sob. "Oh, *no*." Putting the cleanser in the little coaster she kept for just that purpose, she headed for the living room with sponge and Glamorene.

The next time Mrs. Brainerd came she stayed for a scant thirty seconds. She stood in the doorway, sniffing the air. Ambrose had Done It again—twice.

"It really does get out stains even bleach can't reach," Norma said, flourishing the cleanser can.

"Everyone knows that," Clarice Brainerd said, passing it off. Then she sniffed. "This will do wonders for your musty rooms," she said, handing Norma a can of aerosol deodorant, and turned without even coming in and closed the door.

Norma spent four days getting ready for the day she invited Mrs. Brainerd to look into the stove. ("I'm having a little trouble with the bottoms of the open shelves," she confided on the phone. She had just spent days making sure they were immaculate. "I just wondered if you could tell me what to use," she said seductively, thinking that when Clarice Brainerd saw that Norma was worried about dirt in an oven that was cleaner than any oven in the block, she would be awed and dismayed, and she would have to invite Norma to the next day's morning coffee hour.)

At the last minute, Norma had to shoo Polly Ann out of the living room. "I was just making a dress for Ambrose," Polly Ann said, putting on her Mary Janes and picking up her cloth and pins.

Vacuuming frantically, Norma stampeded her down the hall and into her room. "Never *mind*."

"Arient did the job all right," Mrs. Brainerd said, sniffing the air without even pausing to say hello. "The *rest* of us have been using it for years."

"I know," Norma said apologetically.

In the kitchen, she spent a long time with her head in the oven. "I don't think you have too much trouble," she said grudgingly. "In fact it looks real nice. But I would take a pin and clear out those gas jets." Her voice was muffled because of the oven, and for a second Norma had to fight back wild temptation to push her the rest of the way in, and turn on the gas.

Then Clarice said, "It looks real nice. And thanks, I will have some of your cake."

"No greasy feel," Norma said, weak with gratitude. "You'll really sit down for a minute? You'll really have some coffee and sit down?"

"Only for a minute."

Norma got out her best California pottery—the set with the rooster pattern—and within five minutes, she and Mrs. Brainerd were sitting primly in the living room. The organdy curtains billowed and the windows and woodwork shone brightly and for a moment Norma almost imagined that she and Mrs. Brainerd were being photographed in behalf of some product, in *her* living room, and their picture—in full color—would appear in the very next issue of her favorite magazine.

"I would so love to do flower arrangements," Norma said, made bold by her success.

Mrs. Brainerd wasn't listening.

"Maybe join the Garden Club?"

Mrs. Brainerd was looking down. At the rug.

"Or maybe the Music League . . ." Norma looked down, where Mrs. Brainerd was looking, and her voice trailed off.

"Cat hairs," said Mrs. Brainerd. "Loose threads."

"Oh. I *tried* . . ." Norma clapped her hand to her mouth with a muffled wail.

"And scuff marks, on the hall floor . . ." Mrs. Brainerd was shaking her head. "Now, I don't mean to be mean, but if you were to entertain the coffee group, with the house looking like this . . ."

"My daughter was sewing," Norma said faintly. "She *knew* I was having company, but she came in here. It's a little hard," she said, trying to smile engagingly. "When you have kids . . ."

Mrs. Brainerd was on her feet. "The rest of us manage."

Norma managed to keep the sob out of her voice. ". . . and pets . . ."

"The coffee hours," Norma said, maundering. "The garden club . . ."

But Mrs. Brainerd was already gone.

Norma snuffled. "She didn't even mention a *product* to try."

"I made Ambrose a baby carriage," Polly Ann said, dragging Ambrose through in a box. "Is that lady gone?"

"Gone," Norma said, looking at the way the box had scarred her hardwood floor. "She may be gone forever," she said, and began to cry. "Oh Polly Ann, what can we do? We may have to move to a less desirable residential district."

"Ambrose tipped over Puff's sandbox and got You Know What all over the floor." Polly Ann went outside.

Crumbs, hairs, threads, dust all seemed to converge on Norma then, eddying and swirling, threatening, plunging her into blackest despair. She sank to the couch, too overwhelmed to cry and it was then, looking down, that she spied the magazine protruding from under the rug, and things began to change.

END HOUSEHOLD
DRUDGERY,

the advertisement said.

YOUR HOUSE CAN BE
THE CYNOSURE
OF YOUR NEIGHBORHOOD.

Norma wasn't sure what cynosure meant, but there was a picture of a spotless and shining lady, sitting in the middle of a spotless and shining living room, with an immaculate kitchen just visible through a door behind. Trembling with hope, she cut out the accompanying coupon, noting without a qualm that she would have to liquidate the rest of her savings to afford the product, or machine, or whatever it was. Satisfaction was guaranteed and if she got satisfaction it was worth it, every cent of it.

It was unprepossessing enough when it came.

It was a box, small and corrugated, and inside, wrapped in excelsior, was a small, lavender enamel-covered machine. A nozzle and hose, also lavender, were attached. Curious, Norma began leafing through the instruction book, and as she read she began to smile, because it all became quite plain.

"EFFECTS ARE NOT NECESSARILY PERMANENT, "She read aloud, to assuage her conscience. "CAN BE REVERSED BY USING GREEN GAUGE ON THE MACHINE. Oh, Puff," she called, thinking of the white angora hairs which had sullied so many rugs. "Puffy, come here."

The cat came through the door with a look of insolence.

"Come here," Norma said, aiming the nozzle. "Come on, baby," she said, and when Puff approached, she switched on the machine.

A pervasive hum filled the room, faint but distinct.

Expensive or not it was worth it. She had to admit that none of her household cleansers worked as fast. In less than a second Puff was immobile—walleyed and stiff-backed but immobile, looking particularly fluffy and just as natural as life. Norma arranged the cat artistically in a corner by the TV set and then went looking for Polly Ann's dog. She made Ambrose sit up and beg and just as he snapped for the puppy-biscuit she turned on the machine and ossified him in a split-second. When it was over she propped him on the other side of the television set and carefully put away the machine.

Polly Ann cried quite a bit at first.

"Now, honey, if we ever get tired of them this way, we can reverse the machine and let them run around again. But right now, the house is so *clean*, and see how cute they are? They can see and hear everything you want them to," she said, quelling the child's sticky tears. "And look, you can dress Ambrose up all you want, and he won't even squirm."

"I guess so," Polly Ann said, smoothing the front of her velvet dress. She gave Ambrose a little poke.

"And see how little dirt they make."

Polly Ann bent Ambrose's paw in a salute. It stayed. "Okay, Momma. I guess you're right."

Mrs. Brainerd thought the dog and cat were very cute. "How did you *get* them to stay so still?"

"New product," Norma said with a smug smile, and then she wouldn't tell Mrs. Brainerd what product. "I'll get my cake now," she said. "No greasy feel."

"No greasy feel," Mrs. Brainerd said automatically, echoing her, and almost smiled in anticipation.

Moving regally, proud as a queen, Norma brought her coffee tray into the living room. "Now about the coffee hour," she said, presuming because Mrs. Brainerd took up her cup and spoon with an almost admiring look, poking with her fork at the chocolate cake. ("I got the stainless with coupons. You know the kind.")

"The coffee hours," Mrs. Brainerd said, almost mesmerized. Then, looking down, "Oh, what on earth is that?"

And already dreading what she would see, Norma followed Mrs. Brainerd's eyes.

There was a puddle, a distinct puddle, forming under the bathroom door, and as the women watched it, it massed and began making a sticky trail down the highly polished linoleum of the hall.

"I'd better . . ." Mrs. Brainerd said, getting up.

"I know," Norma said with resignation. "You'd better go." Then, as she rose and saw her neighbor to the door, she stiffened with a new resolve. "You just come back tomorrow. I can promise you, everything just as neat as pie." Then, because she couldn't help herself, "No greasy feel."

"You know," Mrs. Brainerd said ominously, "This kind of thing can only go on for so long. My time is valuable. There are the coffee hours, and the Canasta group..."

"I promise you," Norma said. "You'll envy my way with things. You'll tell all your friends. Just come back tomorrow. I'll be ready, I promise you..."

Clarice deliberated, unconsciously fingering her Good Luck earrings with one carefully groomed hand. "Oh," she said finally, after a pause which left Norma in a near faint from anxiety. "All right."

"You'll see," Norma said to the closing door. "Wait and see if you don't see."

Then she made her way through the spreading pool of water and knocked on the bathroom door.

"I was making Kool-Ade to sell to all the Daddies," Polly Ann said, gathering all the overflowing cups and jars.

"Come with me, baby," Norma said. "I want you to get all cleaned up and in your very best clothes."

They were all arranged very artistically in the living room, the dog and the cat curled next to the sofa, Polly Ann looking just as pretty as life in her maroon velvet dress with the organdy pinafore. Her eyes were a little glassy and her legs did stick out at a slightly unnatural angle, but Norma had thrown an afghan over one end of the couch, where she was sitting, and thought the effect, in the long run, was just as good as anything she'd ever seen on a television commercial, and almost as pretty as some of the pictures she had seen in magazines. She noticed with a little pang that there was a certain moist look about the way Polly Ann was watching her, and so she went to the child and patted one waxen hand.

"Don't you worry, honey. When you get big enough to help Momma with her housecleaning, Momma will let you run around for a couple of hours every day. Momma promises."

Then, smoothing the front of her Swirl housedress and refastening her Sweetheart pin, she went to meet Mrs. Brainerd at the door.

"Well," said Mrs. Brainerd in an almost good-natured way. "How nice everything looks."

"No household odor, no stains, no greasy feel to the cake," said Norma anxiously. "This is my little girl."

"What a good child," Mrs. Brainerd said, skirting Polly Ann's legs, which stuck straight out from the couch.

"And our doggy and kitty," Norma said with growing confidence, propping Ambrose against one of Polly Ann's feet because he had begun to slide.

Mrs. Brainerd even smiled. "How cute. How nice."

"Come see the darling kitchen," Norma said, standing so Clarice Brainerd could look into the unclogged drain, the white and pristine sink.

"Just lovely," Clarice said.

"Let me get the cake and coffee," Norma said, leading Clarice Brainerd back to the living room.

"Your windows are just sparkling."

"I know," Norma said, beaming and capable.

"And the rug."

"Glamorene."

"Wonderful." Clarice was hers.

"Here," Norma said, plying her with coffee and cake.

"Wonderful coffee," Clarice said. "Call me Clarice. Now about the Garden Club, and the morning coffee hours . . . We go to Marge on Thursday, and Edna Mondays, and Thelma Tuesday afternoons, and . . ." She bit into the proffered piece of cake. "And . . ." she said, turning the morsel over and over in her mouth.

"And . . ." Norma said hopefully.

"And . . ." Mrs. Brainerd said, looking slightly cross-eyed down her nose, as if she were trying to see what was in her mouth. "This cake," she said. "This cake . . ."

"Marvel Mix," Norma said with elan. "No greasy feel . . ."

"I'm sorry," Mrs. Brainerd said, getting up.

"You're—*what*?"

"Sorry," Mrs. Brainerd said, with genuine regret. "It's your cake."

"What about my cake?"

"Why, it's got that greasy feel."

"You—I—it—but the commercial *promised* . . ." Norma was on her feet now, moving automatically. "The cake is so good, and my house is so beautiful . . ." She was in between Mrs. Brainerd and the door now, heading her off in the front hall.

"Sorry," Mrs. Brainerd said. "I won't be seeing you. Now, if you'll just close that closet door, so I can get by . . ."

"Close the door?" Norma's eyes were glazed. "I can't. I have to get something off the closet shelf."

"It doesn't matter what you get," Mrs. Brainerd said. "I can't come back. We ladies have so much to do, we don't have time . . ."

"Time," Norma said, getting what she wanted from the shelf.

"Time," Mrs. Brainerd said condescendingly. "Oh. Maybe you'd better not call me Clarice."

"Okay, Clarice," Norma said, and she let Mrs. Brainerd have it with the lavender machine.

First she propped Mrs. Brainerd up in a corner, where she would be uncomfortable. Then she reversed the nozzle action and brought Polly Ann and Puff and Ambrose back to mobility. Then she brought her box of sewing scraps and all the garbage from the kitchen, and began spreading the mess around Mrs. Brainerd's feet and she let Puff rub cat hairs on the furniture and she sent Polly Ann into the back yard for some mud. Ambrose, released, Did It at Mrs. Brainerd's feet.

"So glad you could come, Clarice," Norma said, gratified by the look of horror in Mrs. Brainerd's trapped and frozen face. Then, turning to Polly Ann's laden pinafore, she reached for a handful of mud.

Across the Bar

In her youth Maud Constable had talked longingly about the days when she would be a venerable widow with beautiful white hair; she would live like a small gem in an exquisitely furnished setting well away from spilled cereal and greasy fingerprints, and in solitude she would perfect her poetry. She secretly knew she would never really be any better than she was but she used this fiction to prepare herself for the eventual loss of her children to adult life and for the unbearable prospect of outliving her husband.

At seventy-five she was in fact a venerable widow with beautiful white hair, she had an exquisitely furnished apartment in which the walls were white and everything else was rococo and, while she would not admit it, her poetry had in fact grown richer, but the days tasted flat in her mouth and she opened the doors to everybody who came, welcoming dirty feet and fingerprints and fifteen-year-old runaways and assorted deadbeats sleeping curled up in corners, secretly hoping that eventually, one of these mornings, somebody might even spill a bowl of cereal, so that it would be more or less like old times.

When the telegram came, she thought at first that it must be for Anderson, who lived in the dinette, and she went in and cleared her throat to wake him, saying: "Greetings . . ." But when he extended a hand from under the walnut table and took the wire and read it, he scrambled out in a hurry, saying, "Read it again, honey, it's for you."

Her hands were trembling so that she couldn't make out any of the print but she already had the wire by heart:

> GET AFFAIRS IN ORDER.
> NEED YOU FOR SPACE PROBE.

And in the next minute the man from NASA was at the door to explain. Errol and Stanley took Maud into the bedroom to dress for the interview, while Anderson cleared Billy and the cats off the couch so the man from NASA would have a place to sit down. In a minute or two Errol and Stanley opened the bedroom door and Maud sailed out in black, she had put on something that could pass for a cassock, and her white hair made an aureole under the Spanish veil. She looked a little tremulous but her chin was firm, and as she sat down with the man from NASA she gave the others such a look that they cleared the room so she and the man from NASA could be alone.

"Of course," Darrel said at the party Anderson gave to celebrate. "It's the most logical thing in the world."

Mary del Val stopped doing his nails. "But *NASA*."

"They've been talking about it for years," Darrel said, "but there wasn't a poet alive who could pass the physical."

Mary said, "But *Maud*."

Darrel overrode him. "The only person who ever said anything decent in space was Yuri what's-his-name, you know, 'I am iggle.' It's her patriotic duty as a poet."

"Maud's hundred and twelve if she's a day."

"I happen to be seventy-five," Maud said, giving Mary a stuffed grape leaf. "Besides, that's just the point."

Mary sniffed. "Sweetie, you'll disintegrate."

"Oh, but I'll keep on sending, right up to the end. 'Deathsong in the Stars.' "

"Heroic."

"Beautiful."

"I didn't think it was bad," Maud said. "Not half bad at all."

Mary put an arm around her. "Well all right, but we're going to miss you."

"Somebody will put up a statue."

Darrel said, "They might even put you on a stamp."

Mary sighed grudgingly. "Well, I suppose there are *worse* ways to go."

When all the guests had left, Anderson and Billy and Errol and everybody seemed to disappear at the same time; Anderson mumbled something about taking back the deposit bottles and vanished into the night; Billy was already asleep on the couch, and Errol curled tightly in his corner and snored heavily when Maud asked him to take out the garbage, so that she ended, as she always did, by cleaning up after the party all by herself.

Emptying ashtrays and putting lemon wax on all the drink rings, Maud gave considerable thought to what she would wear on the trip. She supposed comfort was an important factor, but after all, this was her triumphal final appearance and she owed posterity something. She thought of herself as dead, sailing in perpetual orbit, and knew she would have to look her best. Besides they had asked her to make a little speech from the gantry for the benefit of all those who would come down to watch the launching and all those billions who would be watching on their screens at home. She thought at first they would expect a white coverall or a lamé jumpsuit with the national emblem stitched across the back, but she had never been at her best in pants. Instead she would wear what she always wore for readings and state occasions—the wine-colored velvet with the lace fichu and the matching mitts. As a concession to the patriotic character of the proceedings she would wear a red-white-and-blue ribbon on a proud diagonal across her breast.

She collected the last of the dirty glasses and, in consideration for her sleeping deadbeats, left the vacuum in its closet and used a handbrush to get up the crumbs. The windows were showing grey daylight when she finished, and she turned off the last of the lamps and sat in the morning shadows, trying hard to think.

There was something wrong with the arrangement, Maud knew it, but she couldn't put her finger on it. Why, for instance, had the man from NASA tactfully suggested that she might want to write at least part of her "Deathsong" *before* she blasted off? Why had he been so indifferent to the idea of physical examinations, or flight training, why had he turned away certain of her questions with a knowing, sympathetic smile?

She would not be back, she already knew that, and it didn't bother her; it was little enough to give in exchange for the chance to write about the stars. She would sing her last song and then blaze into death, grander than any queen on a pyre. She would welcome death, she had wished for it often, she was old and ready to be released from her body; she would join her husband, wherever he was.

Still, all was not what it appeared to be. There were certain things unexplained; she was to be the poet, but she would not be alone on the trip. Who else was going, and why? The man from NASA had smiled and would not say. Wouldn't it take the NASA people a long time to prepare her and the others, whoever they were?

Shouldn't they all be having tests and whirling around in the centrifuge? Apparently not; takeoff would be in just three days, so that she didn't have much time to worry, or to think. Why didn't they want her to have more time to think? Because she might chicken out.

"I won't chicken out," she said firmly. Then she dropped an afghan over the sleeping Billy and went on in to bed.

Emerson woke her at ten to say goodbye. Emerson was her eldest, the vice-president of a bank. He had his secretary get her on the line.

"Mother," he said, "are you out of your mind?"

"Oh," she said. "You've heard."

"The Poet Laureate of Outer Space *indeed*."

"Why Emerson, that's rather nice. Did you make it up?"

"Of course not, Mother. It's in all the papers."

"Well, yes. I thought that was a little imaginative of you."

She could hear Emerson shuffling and rustling at the other end of the phone. She wondered if he had written a speech. He cleared his throat.

"Now Mother, Sam and Andrew and I have been talking, and we want you to reconsider. You only have one life you know, and this . . . this is *undignified*."

Maud sighed. "I suppose you have something better to propose?"

"Well, we decided maybe you weren't getting out enough, and we want to give you a trip to the Bahamas. Three months, if you'd like, expenses paid. And after that—"

"Yes, Emerson?"

"Well, you could spend a month with Sam and one with Andrew and then maybe you could come to Madge and me for Christmas, and after that—"

"Christmas."

"Well you know we'd love to have you for longer, but . . ."

"I don't think so, thank you, Emerson. Thank Sam and Andrew for me, and tell them both goodbye..."

"Have it your way," he said at last, in his it's-your-funeral voice, "but don't expect us at the launching."

"I wouldn't dream of it," Maud said. When she hung up, she felt released.

The morning of the launching everybody got up at four so they could go down to the space installation with her. Darrel and Errol had decorated a delivery truck with bunting and wired in a tape recorder and two loudspeakers with the Triumphal March from *Aida* playing full blast on a continuous loop. Everybody had on his best, which meant tails for Darrel and Errol and a formal for Mary and a poncho for Billy, Guatemalan, hand-woven, and Anderson had shaved for the first time since Maud had known him and was wearing a shiny blue gabardine suit. Someone else had on some kind of uniform, unspecified, but with plenty of gold braid and epaulets, and a couple of the girls from the neighborhood had found jumpsuits somewhere and altered them to fit like wallpaper, with intriguing cutouts over the cleavage and at the waist.

It was an ungodly hour, but everybody was in a wonderful mood. Anderson had taken every whisky and liqueur in Maud's cabinet and made a punch, and Darrel and Mary had spent the whole preceding day baking a cake in the shape of a launching pad with a spun sugar rocket with the name Maud on it taking off in a cloud of cotton candy with candles placed strategically around the blastoff area.

Maud rode in front with Anderson, who was driving, while everybody laughed and sang and popped balloons and rolled around together in the back.

Anderson said, "I'll take care of the plants while you're gone. What do you want me to do with the cats?"

"If you can't find good homes for them, I suppose you'd better have them put away."

"Maud, you're going to want them when you get back."

"You know I won't be back." When he wouldn't look at her, she began rummaging in her beaded bag. She found a wad of papers and pressed it on him. "Look, I've written part of the 'Deathsong', I want you to hang on to it."

"But you'll be transmitting it from space."

"This is only the first canto," Maud said. "I want something to live after me In Case."

He didn't want to take it, but she made him. He wouldn't voice any doubts about the trip, if he gave in to his doubts he would have to turn the truck around and take them all back home. Instead he said, "Maud, we're all very proud of you."

When they got to the launching area they discovered several things all at once. There were ten other people, all about Maud's age, along with their families, all jostling outside the portal; when they went through the portal, all their friends and relations would have to stay outside, they would have to watch the launching on a monitor. So they learned Maud would not be alone on the flight, and they learned that the project had a name: it was to be called Operation Hope. When some twenty more old people had gathered and everybody was milling in suspense, a second lieutenant came out and gave an embarrassed little speech.

They were all welcome, they were pioneers in a new project; one of the nation's scientists had discovered that under certain conditions, zero gravity could retard the aging process, and so this first valiant handful might stay young forever in free fall; they would pave the way for billions to new and extended lives. Maud was the poet laureate and chronicler; Maud would give her valedictory at the gantry just before they loaded the ship and propelled the aging, valiant crew into their greatest adventure. It was Maud who would write their names in the stars and trail their message into the reaches of space.

When Maud said goodbye at the portal, Darrel and Errol fell on each other's necks and cried. Mary was trying to be brave, but she had long since retreated behind sunglasses and wouldn't speak for fear of losing control.

Anderson said, "Why won't they tell us more? Why can't we come in to watch?"

"You'll see me," Maud said. "I'll light up the sky."

"Oh, Maudie, I don't think we ought to let you go."

"Goodbye dear," she said, and kissed him quickly on the cheek.

Looking over his shoulder, she wondered why nobody else seemed suspicious, why none of the valedictory relatives had asked for any more details, and she understood that nobody cared. Her shipmates were going through the gate quickly, carried along by their families. Sons and daughters and nephews and nieces and grandchildren and a few great-grands were propelling all the old men and women towards the gate, moving inexorably even as they showered farewell hugs and kisses and repeated demands to write. She saw that the old people went uncertainly, their expressions a mixture of apprehension and hope, and she detached herself from her own group quickly, kissing each in turn, and then drew a deep breath at the portal and went inside.

An old man tottered next to her, carrying a cardboard suitcase. "We're going to be young again," he said. "They promised."

A twisted little woman no older than Maud turned to him with an expression of profound bitterness. "Don't be so sure."

Somebody else said, "It doesn't matter. Anything's better than what we have."

Maud said gently, "We're going to see the stars."

"Stars, hell." Maud recognized a man whose children

had pushed him forward and fled before he even reached the gate. "All I wanted was *out* of there."

Someone was crying. "Oh, oh, there are too *many* of us."

Looking ahead, Maud saw that their group was not alone. There must have been thousands of people in their seventies and eighties all coming from different portals, all converging on the ship; they came with satchels and handbags and canvas duffel bags and ancient, wheezing dogs and bird cages with scraggly parakeets, with balls of string and old clippings and pipes and syringes, all the paraphernalia of old age; they came in panama hats and antiquated lace dresses and one or two wore World War I uniforms, shuffling along with leg-bindings flapping and once-sleek coats hanging on their inadequate frames; they came out of despair and apprehension, with their eyes glazed and their lips slightly parted in hope.

There were almost too many of them for the ship; it loomed, some ten blocks high, and if they did all fit, they would never make it off the ground. She looked at the ship and then looked about her at the field of aging folk and she faltered, because she understood.

A strong hand closed on her elbow. "We want you to give a farewell speech from the gantry." It was the lieutenant. "We're very honored to have you aboard, Mrs. Constable." He took a hasty look around. "And we're counting on you to make this the kind of occasion it ought to be."

"Yes," Maud said. "You mean I am the Judas goat."

"We have to get them on the ship somehow," he said and then covered his mouth.

She knew perfectly well what would happen; it was a disposal operation, she could tell from the naked look on the captain's face, the cynical expressions of the crew who bustled around in white coveralls, collecting the old people like cowboys making a cattle drive. She would get to give her speech from the gantry and then they would all load; there might be a Trumpet Voluntary or a chorus of the "Stars and Stripes Forever" before blastoff and then the rocket would explode on the gantry with all hands aboard and the nation would say, How sad, and heave a sigh of relief.

She knew what she could do: she could rise to the platform and cry out Beware, or Help; she could alert the whole nation, they would come to save her and all the others from an ignominious death. She thought of Emerson: would he come? Would they? She realized she had known, she had known from the beginning that she would never get off the ground, and so had some of the rest of them; the outside world may have known it too, perhaps they had known it all along. Considering, she looked at the others rustling about her and she became aware of all their fatigue, their infirmities, the miseries of age and all their accumulated pain, and she hesitated only a second before she looked the lieutenant in the eye and said, "Very well."

Standing between two major generals on the platform draped with bunting, Maud gave a beautiful little speech for Darrel and Errol and Anderson and Mary and all the others who were watching, and especially for all the old people clustered about her feet. For everybody's sake she had to make a graceful exit: her speech would be read into the *Congressional Record*, and in homes all over the nation the great television audience found itself dabbing at its eyes. About her, the old people surged towards the loading platform; now their eyes were bright with hope and they would board the ship with pride.

When Maud had finished she made a small bow: a prayer? and stepped inside.

She could hear all the others behind her, chittering and sighing, but she had no time to speak to them; she had work to do. Instead she withdrew inside herself, sitting docilely where the crewmen put her, obediently setting her arms into the clamps so they could strap her down. She would be dead within the hour, they would all be dead, but she was after all a poet and she would give her remaining minutes to composing the second, the final canto of her never-to-be-published deathsong, a longer narrative poem which she had tentatively titled "Across the Bar."

Empty Nest

"The poor dear," said Miss Mahalia Thrip. "The poor, poor, poorpoorpoor dear." Rocking forward on the toes of her multicolored sandals, she strained across the fence. "Are you lonely, dear?"

Prune-wrinkled, birdlike Missus Avis bent over the rich loam in her garden and ignored her. She jammed her sun hat down over her ears and grubbed disconsolately in the dirt.

"She's making a bad adjustment, poor thing," Mahalia Thrip told herself. "Ah well, on to work." Humming breezily, she rocked back on the heels of her multicolored sandals, gathered momentum and strode on.

Mahalia Thrip's multicolored sandals were her only concession to fashion. "A social worker," she always said, "must not attempt to dazzle her clients. People are less inclined to internalize their problems when they're talking to a person who is inconspicuously dressed."

She wore a tan gabardine WAC uniform with the insignia ripped off and a white cotton blouse. She seldom took the jacket off because portions of her strained against the patch pockets of the cotton blouse and wiggled ominously when she walked. Indoors or out, she wore a dark green straw hat dead centered on her forehead. At dead center of the centered hat was a brown plastic scarab. Miss Thrip's clients, washed back by a tidal wave of words, had a way of staring at that scarab, transfixed, and Miss Thrip's own eyes were slightly crossed from trying to glance up at it when she thought no one else was looking.

That day Miss Thrip saw several families, but her heart and her thoughts were with Missus Avis.

"I mean," she said at lunch, "that poor, poor dear is my own neighbor. If a worker can't help her own neighbor make a proper adjustment, she can't be very effective, can she?"

"How long's she lived near you?" the counterman said, swishing his rag at the far end of the lunch counter because he didn't really care about the answer.

"Oh, she's not the one who lives near *me*. I live near *her*. I mean, I just moved in yesterday, and my landlady told me who she was, and she looked so unhappy I just knew there must be something I could do. She looked so—so unassimilated, kneeling out there. You know," (she leaned across the counter earnestly) "old people have such a problem. This being ineffectual seems to get to them—they're old, and they think they're too old for a proper group experience. Why, all they have to do is find the right group!"

She bent over her carrot-and-raisin salad, sloshing her fork in her poached egg before she dug in. "Poor thing, I'll have to do something for her. I really will. I mean, I'd like to help her—I'd like to help her verbalize her problems, and then she'd be on the road to a busy life."

The counterman, who swished with his rag and stacked glasses and piled pieces of bread one on top of the other until there was nothing else to do, had come back to stand in front of his customer.

"You're wonderful to be interested in Missus Avis, young man," said Mahalia Thrip. "But perhaps you're unhappy too; perhaps there's something I—or my agency—could do for you. You know, we like to think people who are well adjusted socially will come to us, to look us over, you might say, just because we're there. You can get my check now, if you will. Young man!"

"Huh? Oh." He had been staring at the scarab.

That afternoon, when she stopped to give the Brintz family the monthly check, she found herself talking about her unhappy neighbor to Mrs. Brintz. With a start, she remembered herself and began again on the problems of Willie Brintz. "Now, if your boy had somebody he could really identify with, if he could . . ." Hypnotized, Mrs. Brintz watched the scarab and made no protest.

Hairy, sweaty, outspoken, outraged Brintz senior surged into the living room. "Whyn' cha shaddup, lady, and give us the dough?"

"You mean your—assistance?"

"Yeah. My ass—istance." Brintz cuffed his wife. "Quit sittin' around here listenin' to her gas, Myrtle. Get back to work."

"Oh, of course." Miss Thrip, meaty jaw thrust forward, stood toe to toe with Brintz. "Of course, you should realize, our counselling is three hundred times as important to you as any check." Brintz took a step forward. "Goodbye, Mr. Brintz. Goodbye, Mrs. Brintz. Remember what I said about Willie . . ."

Preoccupied with her sad-looking neighbor, Miss Thrip hardly listened as Wanda Wentworth spewed forth her troubles. They were the same troubles Wanda Wentworth had been masticating ("verbalizing," Miss Thrip corrected herself) for the past six years.

"Well, if you aren't gonna listen to me, when I'm

tellin' you about this real new insight I got into me and my troubles, I'm gonna quit comin' to you and go to Family Service," Wanda Wentworth huffed. "Crumbum like you thinks you can set up your own social agency. I mean, I got plenty of people dyin' to listen to me. See this list?" (Miss Thrip hardly looked at the woman as she brought out a legal-sized piece of paper crammed with names; she was too preoccupied with Missus Avis.) "Well, these are all the people inna world who are conspirin' against me. An' if you don't wanna listen to me, I'm gonna put you on my list!"

"Um," Miss Thrip said. "Oh, of course, Wanda. That will be fine. Now if you'll try to give me the clarification on your problems a little better next time I see you, I think we'll really get somewhere. Goodbye."

Scarcely breathing hard, Miss Thrip breezed through two mother-in-law problems, one ruptured marriage and a misplaced check, all with her mind fixed on quitting-time, when she could devote her credits in Soc. 101 and Abnormal Psychology 202 and her skilled mind and her ready understanding to the little old lady who grubbed in the garden next door to her new home.

"Good evening, my dear." As springy as she had been nine hours before, Miss Thrip opened the picket gate and bounced up the walk to see Missus Avis.

"Keep away from that door—please!" Busy in the dirt, Missus Avis looked up to deliver the plea. Then she went back to digging white, flaccid things out of the dirt and putting them in a tin can. They looked like worms.

"Going fishing?" Miss Thrip sank on her heavy haunches and began poking companionably at the dirt.

"No. N . . . no!" Missus Avis looked almost frightened.

"Well . . ." Miss Thrip blenched as her hand closed on something soft and squirmy. "Shall we sit on your steps and talk a minute?"

The old lady sighed. "If we got to."

"You—you looked so lonely, sitting out here in your yard, digging all day. I just wondered if you had enough to do."

"I got plenty to do. I got to dig."

"I mean—well, so many of our senior citizens find themselves with time on their hands. One mustn't feel one is unique just because one's hair has begun to run to silver." Miss Thrip giggled at the poetic turn of phrase.

"Hair always has been white. Been white ever since I got married. Don't bother me." Surreptitiously, the old lady let her hand drift off the steps into the dirt, in an automatic search for more worms.

"I don't think you understand, my dear. I mean, there are many people—your age—who simply haven't enough to do. Did you know that there are many organized recreations—really profitable group experiences—for you and others like you? You'd find your whole life enriched if you took the time to put your hand in mine and let me lead you to a happier pattern of group living." Miss Thrip sat back and basked in her eloquence.

"Can't take your hand." The old lady surveyed her fingers, encrusted with heavy loam. "Hands are too dirty."

"You know," Miss Thrip said coyly. "I think you're playing a little game with me. Perhaps I've started at this wrong. Perhaps we should discuss you and your problems. I mean, sometimes our life experiences are so great we find it impossible to verbalize our reactions, unless we are drawn out by experienced counsellors. Now, you say you are married?"

"Was."

"Your husband—passed away?"

"Might say that. He more sorta passed out." The old lady picked up her tin can and began rattling the worms in it. "Right out of the window, 'sa matter of fact." She took out one worm that was undersized and threw it back in the dirt. "Just as well."

"I—ah—gather your life with him was not altogether happy?"

"It was diffrunt." Placidly the old lady clamped the tin can between her knees and began wiping her hands on her skirts. "I got to go in pretty quick."

"Do you—have any children? Perhaps you seem unhappy because you are having problems with your children. Adult children in the home can make many an ol—a senior citizen—feel uncomfortable and even superannuated." Miss Thrip felt she had scored.

"Kids don't live here. Got two—twins. Like to kill me, having 'em, but they're grown now, and I almost forgot how much it hurt."

"They no longer live here? Then perhaps you are alone because the little ones have flown away."

The old lady started and almost dropped her can of worms. "How'j you know?"

"Oh, it's just a syndrome I know," Miss Thrip said with pride. "Tomorrow we'll talk some more, and when you see yourself and your problems in clearer relief, you won't mind coming out for a little recreation with others of your own kind."

"Oh, I couldn't do that." The old lady jumped to her feet, clutching the can of worms to her lean rib-cage. "I got to stay here."

"But why?"

"In case."

"In case?"

"Kids might come. They might come visit. You get outa here now, lady. They might even come tonight."

"I'll be back," Miss Thrip trilled, and she bounded away down the walk.

"You see, it's all perfectly simple," she told the counterman the next day. Her face was flushed with excitement, and her grizzled hair rippled across her pink skull in a new marcel she'd had just to impress the old lady. "It's the universal problem—one of the last life experiences, and one that is so hard for many a poor mother. The kiddies fly away, and all her mothering talent is wasted—it's all been lavished on them for years, and suddenly they are gone, and she has no place to give her bounty. She retreats into herself and refuses to seek happiness with others her own age." Rapt, Miss Thrip forgot even to break her poached egg. "You see, she still dreams that the kiddies are coming back, and until I can make her verbalize that dream—a sort of inner clarification is essential—she won't be able to lead a happy life without doing that. You see—" she leaned forward in a flash of brilliance—"she's waiting beside an empty nest."

Busily, she took out a notebook and scribbled a few sentences. Then she looked at the counterman. "Young man, I said check please!"

"Huh? Oh!" He had been staring at the scarab.

She fairly flew home. She plunged through the picket gate and drew up next to Missus Avis, who had a good day's collection of worms mounded in her tin can.

"Now, perhaps if we talk about it, my dear, you will see how silly it is for you to be spending your time here gardening, when you could be out empathizing with others your own age. "Oh . . ." she flapped her hands exasperatedly. "Can't you put down that dirt?"

"I got to dig."

"Well, if you must. Perhaps this is good therapy for you. Perhaps we could group therapize you. I'm sure there are plenty of garden clubs where you could find companionship and recreation . . ." Miss Thrip smoothed her hands over her gabardine skirt, trying not to notice that Missus Avis was regarding an extremely large worm with particular pride.

"I dig here."

"Ah . . . of course. Well, I was thinking, if you joined a garden club, perhaps you could learn to raise some really beautiful flowers here—things your children would be proud to see, if they should come back to visit their mamma."

"They ain't comin' back. I *hope* they ain't comin' back." Missus Avis had jumped to her feet in a shower of dirt and pale, plump worms. She looked skyward, shielding her head with her arms.

"But you said yesterday that they might come to visit!" Bewildered, Miss Thrip reached for her notebook. "Interesting reaction . . . must note this down . . ."

"Said they might come to visit." The old lady had settled in the dirt again. "Didn't say I wished they would. Hope they never do. Hope to hell they never do."

"Missus Avis!" Shocked, Mahalia Thrip mumbled to herself. A social worker must never make value judgments. Especially on some such integral thing as one's language or one's attitude. One's client is entitled to that attitude. "Oh, Missus Avis, perhaps if you told me about it, my dear . . ."

The old lady had begun to grub in the dirt again, picking up the dropped worms. Now, ignoring Mahalia Thrip's outstretched hand and her confidential, listening attitude, she picked up her can of worms and headed towards her front door. "I got to go in now."

"Perhaps I could come in with you. Often when a worker communicates with a client in her own surroundings, she finds her more at ease. Then you could verbalize . . ."

"I got to go in now. Alone. I got to get a box off to my kids."

"Well . . ." Before Miss Thrip had pocketed her notebook and tucked in the tail of her flimsy cotton blouse, the old lady had turned on her heel and slammed the front door behind her. Miss Thrip resisted the temptation to try the knob.

She had several more interviews in the old lady's garden. She brought enrolment blanks from the garden club and samples from a ceramics class and brochures from the Senior Citizens' Center. She contemplated bringing by an elderly rake from the Senior Citizens' Center, but reconsidered; it might bring back sad memories to the old lady. She sat through countless worm-digging sessions and retained her professional calm. "I got to dig," the old lady said. "I got to dig *here*."

"I can't seem to get close to her," she said to the dictaphone at the end of the week. "I—the case worker finds it difficult to approach the client, who fails to respond to approaches which have succeeded with many others, and refuses to tell all—or anything, for that matter. Perhaps the best solution would be for the worker to drop in unexpectedly, when the client is in her parlor, where she might be able, perhaps, to achieve a closer relationship because of the more intimate environment. Perhaps the only way to do that would be for the worker to go home unexpectedly, say, in the middle of the day, when the client might be in her home, eating lunch. Perhaps, if the worker went now . . ."

Miss Thrip gave herself the rest of the day off.

She took a cab right to the door of the old lady's house, she was so anxious to try her new plan. She paid the cabdriver and resisted an urge to vault the picket gate. Demurely, she swung it open and started up the walk.

The yard was deserted. The windows of the bungalow, a small one which couldn't contain more than one or two rooms and a kitchen, were covered from the inside. The old lady must be in her house. Tentatively, Miss Thrip tapped on the green front door. No answer. She tapped again, and still she heard nothing.

"Perhaps she has gone downtown to mail that package. Perhaps she isn't home at all!" Miss Thrip hummed to herself. "When she returns, she can find me on her living-room couch, looking so natural and at home in her parlor that she won't be able to resist pouring out her whole life story."

Miss Thrip jiggled the handle. The door swung open and she planted one multicolored sandal firmly inside. The floor felt soft. "Hmm, deep-piled rugs," she thought. She moved inside and closed the door. It was dark and her eyes were dazzled by after-images of the sun. She groped for a light switch and flinched as her hand touched something soft and muddy.

She shook her head and her eyes began to clear. She was surprised at the size of the room until she realized there were no inner walls in the house, and that there was only a single room and that the walls of this room were thatched with heavy twigs and daubed with mud and bits of string and had bottles and rocks and bright plastics studded in them like jewels and that the whole room smelled like fetid, feathered death. On the floor were bits of meat and crusts of bread and other pieces of filth that were soft and crawling beneath her feet. The mud-daubed walls made a close circle of the room, where only one spot was bare and clean. In it were a table and a rocking chair and a hammock. Beady-eyed and resentful, the old lady swung in the hammock.

"I told you not to come in. I told you. Don't like my house, do you? Try to keep it just the way the kids left it. Have to. Too bad you don't like it."

"I . . ." Miss Thrip couldn't squeeze out another word.

"Warned you to stay outa here. Said the kids might come back." The old lady cackled. "Didn't think you'd like it—and besides, you better get out of here quick."

"I . . ." Miss Thrip squeaked. She groped for the door and found the handle slippery in her fingers.

"Yep. Told you. Oughta tell you this." The old lady leaned out of her hammock and grinned. "Heard from m'kids. Oldest boy says he's comin' around. Says he's been out courtin'. And you know how boys are when they come home. Always hungry."

"Ak!" Miss Thrip wrenched open the front door and almost tripped on an enormous feather.

She was halfway down the front walk before the shadowy, winged form plummeted down, screaming, to snatch her up.

"Son, son," Missus Avis croaked. "Mind your manners . . ." She ran in circles on the walk, waving her arms at the black blotch roaring towards the sky. "Share with your sister, son!" she screeched. She muttered to herself, kicked the worm can off the front stoop and went back into the empty nest.

In Behalf of the Product

Of course I owe everything I am today to Mr. Manuel Omerta, my personal representative, who arranged for practically everything, including the dental surgery and the annulment, but I want all of you wonderful people to know that I couldn't have done any of it without the help and support of the most wonderful person of all, my Mom. It was Mom who kept coming with the super-enriched formula and the vitamins, she was the one who twirled my hair around her finger every time she washed it, it was Mom who put Vaseline on my eyelashes and paid for the trampoline lessons because she had faith in me. Anybody coming in off the street might have thought I was just an ordinary little girl, but not my mom; why, the first thing I remember is her standing me up on a table in front of everybody. I had on my baby tapshoes and a big smile and Mom was saying, Vonnie is going to be Miss Wonderful Land of Ours someday.

Even then she knew.

Well, here I am, and I can't tell you all how happy I am to be up here, queen of the nation, an inspiration and a model for all those millions and billions of American girls who can grow up to be just like me. And this is only the beginning. Why, after I spend a year touring the country, meeting the people and introducing them to the product, after I walk down the runway at next year's pageant and put the American eagle floral piece into the arms of my successor, and she cries, anything can happen. I might go on to a career as an internationally famous television personality, or if I'd rather, I could become a movie queen or a spot welder, or I could marry Stanley, if he's still speaking to me, and raise my own little Miss Wonderful Land of Ours. Why, the world is mine, except of course for the iron curtain countries and their sympathizers, and after this wonderful year, who knows?

I just wish Daddy could be here to share this moment, but I guess that's just too much to hope, and I want you to know, Daddy, wherever you are out there, I forgive you, and if you'll only turn yourself in and make a public confession, I know the authorities will be lenient with you.

And that goes for you too, Sal. I know it was hard on you, always being the ugly older sister, but I really don't think you should have done what you did, and to show you how big I can be, if the acid scars came out as bad as I think they did, Mom and I are perfectly willing to let bygones be bygones and sink half the prize money into plastic surgery for you. I mean, after all, it's the least we can do. Why, there aren't even any charges outstanding against you; after all, nobody was really hurt— I mean, since Mr. Omerta happened to come in when he did and bumped your arm, and the acid went all over you instead of me.

I know I am the center of all eyes standing up here, I am the envy of millions, and I love the way the silver gown feels, slithering down over me like so much baby oil. I even love the weight of the twenty-foot-long red, white and blue velvet cloak, and every once in a while I want to reach up and touch the rhinestone stars and lightning bolts in my tiara but of course I can't because I am still holding the American eagle floral piece, the emblem of everything I have ever wanted. Of course you girls envy me. I used to get a stomach ache just from looking at the pageant on TV. I would look at the winner smiling out over the Great Seal and I would think: Die, and let it be me. I just want you girls to know it hasn't all been bread and roses, there have been sacrifices, and Mom and Mr. Omerta had to work very hard, so if you're out there watching and thinking: What did she do to deserve that? let me tell you, the answer is, Plenty.

The thing is, without Mr. Omerta, poor Mom and I wouldn't have known where to begin. Before Mr. Omerta, we were just rookies in the ball game of life; we didn't have a prayer. There we were at the locals in the Miss Tiny Miss contest, me in my pink tutu and the little sequined tiara, I even had a wand; it was my first outing and I came in with a fourth runner-up. If it had been up to me I would have turned in my wand right then and there. Maybe Mom would have given up too, if it hadn't been for Mr. Omerta, but there must have been something about me, star quality, because he picked me out of all those other little girls, *me*. He didn't even give the winner a second look, he just came over to us in his elegant kidskin suit and the metallic shoes. We didn't know it then, but it was Mr. Manuel Omerta, and he was going to change my life.

I was a loser, I must have looked a mess; the winner and the first runner-up were over on the platform crying for the camera and pinching each other in between lovey-dovey hugs, it was all over for the day, Mom and I were hanging up our cleats and packing away our uniforms when Mr. Omerta licked Mom's ear and said,

"You two did a lot of things wrong today, but I want to tell you I like your style." I said, Oh, thank you, and went on crying but Mom, she shushed me and hissed at me to listen up. She knew what she was doing too; she wasn't just going to say, Oh, thank you, and take the whole thing sitting down. She said, "What do you mean, a few things wrong?" and Mr. Omerta said, "Listen, I can give you a few pointers. Come over here." I couldn't hear what he said to her but she kept nodding and looking over at me and by the time I went over to tell them they were closing the armory and we had better get out, they were winding up the agreement; Mr. Omerta said, "And I'll only take fifty percent."

"Don't you fifty-percent me," Mom said. "You know she's got the goods or you never would have picked her."

"All right," he said, "forty-five percent."

Mom said, "She has naturally curly hair."

"You're trying to ruin me."

First Mr. Omerta pretended to walk out on Mom and then Mom pretended to take me away and they finally settled it; he would become my personal representative, success guaranteed, and he would take forty-two point eight percent off the top. "The first thing," he said, "Tap dancing is a lousy talent. No big winner has ever made it on tap dancing alone. You have to throw in a gimmick, like pantomime. Something really different."

"Sword swallowing," Mom said, in a flash.

"Keep coming, I really like your style." They bashed it back and forth for another few minutes. "Another thing," Mr. Omerta said. "We've got to fix those teeth; they look kind of, I don't know, *foreign*."

Mom said, "Got it. Mr. Omerta, I think we're going to make a winning team."

It turned out Mr. Omerta was more or less between things and besides, to do a good job he was going to have to be on the spot, so he ended up coming home with us. Dad was a little surprised at first but he got used to it, or at least he acted like he was used to it; he only yelled first thing in the morning, while Sal and I were still hiding in our beds and Mr. Omerta was still out on the sun porch with the pillow over his head, stacking Zs. We fixed the sun porch up for Mr. Omerta; the only inconvenience was when you wanted to watch TV you had to go in and sit on the end of the Hide-a-Bed and sometimes it made him mad and other times it didn't; you were in trouble either way. Sal used to hit him on the knuckles with her leg brace; she said if you just kept smacking him he would get the idea and quit. He didn't bother me much. I was five at the time, and later on I was, you know, the Property; in the end I was going to be up against the Virginity Test and even when you passed that they did a lot of close checking to be sure you hadn't been fooling around. If you are going to represent this Wonderful Land of Ours, you have to be a model for all American womanhood; I mean, you wouldn't put pasties on Columbia the Gem of the Ocean or photograph the Statue of Liberty without her concrete robe, which is why I am so grateful to Mr. Omerta for busting in on Stanley and me in Elkton, Maryland, even if we *were* legally married by a justice of the peace. We could have taken care of the married part, but there was the other thing; it isn't widely known but if you flunk the Test in the semifinals you are tied to the Great Seal in front of everybody and all the other contestants get to cast the first stone.

I cried but Mr. Omerta said not to be foolish, I was only engaging in the classic search for daddy anyway, just like in all the books. I suppose he was right, except that by the time Stanley and I ran away together Daddy had been gone for ten years. We were sitting around one night when I was eight. I had just won the state Miss Subteen title and Mr. Omerta and Mom were clashing glasses; before he put the prize check less his percentage into my campaign fund, Mr. Omerta had lost his head and bought us a couple of bottles of pink champagne. Then Daddy got fed up or something, he threw down his glass and stood up, yelling; "You're turning my daughter into a Kewpie doll." Sally started giggling and Mom slapped her and let my father have it all in one fluid motion. She said, "Henry, it's the patriotic thing to do." He said, "I don't see what that has to do with anything, and besides . . ."

I got terribly quiet. Mom and Mr. Omerta were both leaning forward, saying, "Besides?"

I tried to shut him up but it was too late.

"Besides, what's so wonderful about a country that lets this kind of thing go on?"

"Oh, *Daddy*," I cried, but it was already too late. Mr. Omerta was already on the hot line to the House Un-American Activities Committee Patrol Headquarters; he didn't even hear Daddy yelling that the whole thing was a gimmick to help sell the war. By that time we could hear sirens. Daddy crashed through the back window and landed in the flower bed and that was the last anybody ever saw of him.

Well, we do have to go and visit the troops a lot and we do lead those victory rallies as part of our public appearance tour in behalf of the product, but it's not anything like Daddy said. I mean, any girl would do as much, and if you happen to be named Miss Wonderful Land of Ours, it's an honor and a privilege. I keep dreaming that when I start my nationwide personal appearance tour I will find Daddy standing in the audience in Detroit or Nebraska, he will be carrying a huge UP AMERICA sign and I can take him to my bosom and forgive him and he'll come back home to live.

Now that I think about it, Stanley does look a little bit like Daddy, and maybe that's why I was attracted to him. I mean, it's no fun growing up in a household where there are no men around, unless, of course, you want to count Mr. Omerta, who did keep saying he wanted to be a father to me, but that wasn't exactly what he meant. I was allowed to go to public high school so I could be a cheerleader because that can make or break you if you're going for Miss Teen-Age Wonderful Land of Ours, which of course is only a way station, but it's a lot of good personal experience. As it turned out I only got to the state finals. I could have gone to the nationals as an alternate but Mr. Omerta said it would be bad exposure and besides, we made enough out of the state contest to see us through until it was time for the main event. Anyway, Stanley was captain of the football team the year I made head cheerleader, and at first Mr. Omerta encouraged us because he could take pictures of us sitting in the local soda fountain, one soda and two straws, or me handing a big armful of goldenrod to Stanley after the big game. The thing I liked about Stanley, he wasn't interested in One Thing Only, he really loved me for my soul. When I came in after a date Mr. Omerta would sneak upstairs and sit on the end of my bed in his bathrobe while I told him all about it; you would have thought we were college roommates after the junior prom. Stanley loved me so much I know he would have waited but I decided there were more important things than being Miss Wonderful Land of Ours so the night of graduation we ran off to Elkton, Maryland, and if Mr. Omerta had got there five minutes later it would have been too late.

Whatever you might think about what he did to Stanley, you've got to give him credit for doing his job. He was my personal representative, he got me through the Miss Preteen and the Miss Adolescent with flying colours, and saw me through Miss Teen-Age Wonderful Land of Ours; he got me named Miss Our Town and it was all only a matter of time, I was a cinch for Miss State, and once I got to the nationals, well, with my talent gig, I was a natural, but here I was in Elkton, Maryland, I was just about to throw it all away for a pot of marriage when Mr. Omerta came crashing in and saved the day. What happened was, I was just melting into Stanley's arms when the door banged open and there were about a hundred people in the room, Mr. Omerta in the vanguard. I could have killed him then and there and he knew it. He took me by the shoulders and he looked me in the eye and said, "Brace up, baby, you owe it to your country. I will not let you smirch yourself before the pageant. Death before dishonor," Mr. Omerta said, and then he yelled, "There he is, grab him," and they dragged poor Stanley away. I'll never know how he managed to tail us, but he had the propaganda squad with him and before I could do a thing they had poor Stanley arrested on charges of menacing a national monument, they threw in a couple of perversion charges so Mr. Omerta could push through the annulment, and now poor Stanley is on ice until the end of next year. By that time my tour as Miss Wonderful Land of Ours will be over and maybe Mr. Omerta will let bygones be bygones and clear Stanley's name so he and I can get married again; after all, that's the only way I will ever be eligible to become *Mrs*. Wonderful Land of Ours, and you can't let yourself slip into retirement just because you've already been to the top.

But I haven't told you anything about my talent. I mean, it's possible to take lessons in Frankness and Sincerity, but talent is the one thing you can't fake. Mr. Omerta told us right off that tap dancing alone just wouldn't make it, but every time I tried sword swallowing (Mom's idea) I gagged and had to stop, but the trouble with fire eating was that the first time I burned my face, so naturally after that they couldn't even get me to try tapping and twirling the flaming baton. We thought about pantomime but of course that would rule out the tap and just then Mr. Omerta had an inspiration: he got me an accordion. So I went into the Miss Tiny Miss contest the next year tapping and playing the accordion, but there was a girl who sang patriotic songs and tapped the V for Victory in Morse code, and that gave Mr. Omerta an even better idea. To make a long story short, when I got up here tonight to do my talent for the last time, it was a routine we have been working on for years, and I owe it all to Mr. Omerta, with an extra little bow for Mom, whose idea it was to dress me in the Betsy Ross costume with the cutouts and the skirt ripped off at the crotch, our tattered forefathers and all that, and if you all enjoyed my interpretation of "O Beautiful for Spacious Skies" done in song and dance and pantomime with interludes on the accordion, I want to say a humble thank you, thank you one and all.

I guess not many of you wonderful people know how close I came to not making it. First there was that terrible moment in the semifinals when we went back to find that my entire pageant wardrobe had been stolen, but I want you to know that Miss Massachusetts has been apprehended and they made her give me her wardrobe because between the ripping and the ink she had more or less ruined mine, and I have begged them to go easy on her because we are all working under such a terrible strain. And then there was the thing where they wouldn't let my mom into the rehearsals but they settled that very nicely and she is watching right now from her own private room in the hospital and they will let her come home as soon as she is able to relate. Thanks for everything, Mom, and as soon as we get off TV I'm coming over and give you a great big kiss even if you don't know it's me. Then there's the thing about Mr. Omerta, and I feel just terrible, but it had to be done. I mean, he just snapped last night, he got past all the chaperones and came up to my hotel room. I said, "Oh, Mr. Omerta, you shouldn't *be* here, I could be disqualified," and the next thing I knew he had thrown himself down on my feet. He said, "Vonnie, I love you, I adore you." It was disgusting. He said, "Throw it all over and run away with me." Well, there I was not twenty-four hours from the big title; it was terrible. I said, "Oh, come on, Mr. Omerta, don't start that now, not after what you did to Stanley," and when he wouldn't stop kissing my ankles I kicked him a couple of times and said, "Come on, all you've ever thought about is money, money," and when he said there were more important things than money I started screaming, "Help me, somebody come and help me, this man is making an indecent advance," and the matrons came like lightning and carried him off to jail. Well, what did he expect? He's spent the last thirteen years training me for this day.

So when the big moment came tonight I was the one with the perfect figure, the perfect walk, the perfect talent, I wowed them in the charm department and . . . I don't know, there has just been this guy up here, the All-American Master of Ceremonies; you thought he was kissing my cheek and handing me another bouquet but instead he was whispering in my ear, "OK, sweetie, enough's enough." There seems to be something wrong; it turns out I am not reaching you wonderful people out there, my subjects. You can see my lips moving but that's not me you hear on the PA system, it's a prerecorded speech. He says . . . he says I'm perfect in almost every respect but there's this one thing wrong, they found out too late so they're going to have to go through with it. I guess they found out when I got up here and tried to make this speech. I am a weeny bit too frank to be a typical Miss Wonderful Land of Ours, he says I have too many regrets, but just as soon as I get down from here and they run the last commercial, they're going to take care of that. He says I'll be ready to begin my nationwide personal appearance tour in behalf of the product just as soon as they finish the lobotomy.

The Attack of the Giant Baby

New York City, 9 a.m. Saturday, Sept. 16, 197-: Dr. Jonas Freibourg is at a particularly delicate point in his experiment with electrolytes, certain plant moulds and the man within. Freibourg (who, like many scientists, insists on being called Doctor although he is in fact a Ph.D.) has also been left in charge of Leonard, the Freibourg baby, while Dilys Freibourg attends her regular weekly class in Zen Cookery. Dr. Freibourg has driven in from New Jersey with Leonard, and now the baby sits on a pink blanket in a corner of the laboratory. Leonard, aged fourteen months, has been supplied with a box of Malomars and a plastic rattle; he is supposed to play quietly while Daddy works.
9:20: Leonard has eaten all the Malomars and is tired of the rattle; he leaves the blanket, hitching along the laboratory floor. Instead of crawling on all fours, he likes to pull himself along with his arms, putting his

weight on his hands and hitching in a semi-sitting position.

9:30: Dr. Freibourg scrapes an unsatisfactory culture out of the petridish. He is not aware that part of the mess misses the bin marked for special disposal problems, and lands on the floor.

9:30½: Leonard finds the mess, and like all good babies investigating foreign matter, puts it in his mouth.

9:31: On his way back from the autoclave, Dr. Freibourg trips on Leonard. Leonard cries and the doctor picks him up.

"Whussamadda, Lennie, whussamadda, there, there, what's that in your mouth?" Something crunches. "Ick ick, spit it out, Lennie, Aaaaaaa, Aaaaaaaa, AAAAAAAA."

At last the baby imitates its father: "Aaaaaaa."

"That's a good boy, Lenny, spit it into Daddy's hand, that's a *good* boy, yeugh." Dr. Freibourg scrapes the mess off the baby's tongue. "Oh, yeugh, Malomar, it's okay, Lennie, OK?"

"Ggg.nnn. K." The baby ingests the brown mess and then grabs for the doctor's nose and tries to put that in his mouth.

Despairing of his work, Dr. Freibourg throws a cover over his experiment, stashes Leonard in his stroller and heads across the hall to insert his key in the self-service elevator, going down and away from the secret laboratory. Although he is one block from Riverside Park it is a fine day and so Dr. Freibourg walks several blocks east to join the other Saturday parents and their charges on the benches in Central Park.

10:15: The Freibourgs reach the park. Although he has some difficulty extracting Leonard from the stroller, Dr. Freibourg notices nothing untoward. He sets the baby on the grass. The baby picks up a discarded tennis ball and almost fits it in his mouth.

10:31: Leonard is definitely swelling. Everything he has

on stretches, up to a point: T-shirt, knitted diaper, rubber pants, so that, seen from a distance, he may still deceive the inattentive eye. His father is deep in conversation with a pretty divorcée with twin poodles, and although he checks on Leonard from time to time, Dr. Freibourg is satisfied that the baby is safe.

10:35: Leonard spots something bright in the bushes on the far side of the clearing. He hitches over to look at it. It is, indeed, the glint of sunlight on the fender of a moving bicycle and as he approaches it recedes, so he has to keep approaching.

10:37: Leonard is gone. It may be just as well because his father would most certainly be alarmed by the growing expanse of pink flesh to be seen between his shrinking T-shirt and the straining waistband of his rubber pants.

10:50: Dr. Freibourg looks up from his conversation to discover that Leonard has disappeared. He calls.

"Leonard. Lennie."

10:51: Leonard does not come.

10:52: Dr. Freibourg excuses himself to hunt for Leonard.

11:52: After an hour of hunting, Dr. Freibourg has to conclude that Leonard hasn't just wandered away, he is either lost or stolen. He summons park police.

1 p.m.: Leonard is still missing.

In another part of the park, a would-be mugger approaches a favorite glen. He spies something large and pink: it half-fills the tiny clearing. Before he can run, the pink phenomenon pulls itself up, clutching at a pine for support, topples, and accidentally sits on him.

1:45: Two lovers are frightened by unexplained noises in the woods, sounds of crackling brush and heavy thuddings accompanied by a huge, wordless maundering. They flee as the thing approaches, gasping out their stories to an incredulous policeman who detains them until the ambulance arrives to take them to Bellevue.

At the sound of what they take to be a thunder crack,

THE ATTACK OF THE GIANT BABY

a picnicking family returns to the picnic site to find their food missing, plates and all. They assume this is the work of a bicycle thief but are puzzled by a pink rag left by the marauder: it is a baby's shirt, stretched beyond recognition and ripped as if by a giant, angry hand.

2 p.m.: Extra units join park police to widen the search for missing Leonard Freibourg, aged fourteen months. The baby's mother arrives and after a pause for recriminations leaves her husband's side to augment the official description: that was a sailboat on the pink shirt, and those are puppy-dogs printed on the Carter's dress-up rubber pants. The search is complicated by the fact that police have no way of knowing the baby they are looking for is not the baby they are going to find.

4:45: Leonard is hungry. Fired by adventure, he has been chirping and happy up till now, playing doggie with a stray Newfoundland which is the same relative size as his favorite stuffed Scottie at home. Now the Newfoundland has used its last remaining strength to steal away, and Leonard remembers he is hungry. What's more, he's getting cranky because he has missed his nap. He begins to whimper.

4:45 1/60: With preternatural acuity, the distraught mother hears. "It's Leonard," she says.

At the sound, park police break out regulation slickers and cap covers, and put them on. One alert patrolman feels the ground for tremors. Another says, "I'd put up my umbrella if I was you, lady, there's going to be a helluva storm."

"Don't be ridiculous," Mrs. Freibourg says. "It's only Leonard, I'd know him anywhere." Calls. "Leonard, it's Mommy."

"I don't know what it is, lady, but it don't sound like any baby."

"Don't you think I know my own child?" She picks up a bullhorn. "Leonard, it's me, Mommy. Leonard, Leonard . . ."

From across the park, Leonard hears.

5 p.m.: The WNEW traffic control helicopter reports a pale, strange shape moving in a remote corner of Central Park. Because of its apparent size, nobody in the helicopter links this with the story of the missing Freibourg baby. As the excited reporter radios the particulars and the men in the control room giggle at what they take to be the first manifestations of an enormous hoax, the mass begins to move.

5:10: In the main playing area, police check their weapons as the air fills with the sound of crackling brush and the earth begins to tremble as something huge approaches. At the station houses nearest Central Park on both East and West sides, switchboards clog as apartment-dwellers living above the tree line call in to report the incredible thing they've just seen from their front windows.

5:11: Police crouch and raise riot guns; the Freibourgs embrace in anticipation; there is a hideous stench and a sound as if of rushing wind and a huge shape enters the clearing, carrying bits of trees and bushes with it and gurgling with joy.

Police prepare to fire.

Mrs. Freibourg rushes back and forth in front of them, protecting the huge creature with her frantic body. "Stop it you monsters, it's my baby."

Dr. Freibourg says, "My baby. Leonard," and in the same moment his joy gives way to guilt and despair. "The culture. Dear heaven, the beta culture. And I thought he was eating Malomars."

Although Leonard has felled several small trees and damaged innumerable automobiles in his passage to join his parents, he is strangely gentle with them. "M.m.m.m.m.m," he says, picking up first his mother and then his father. The Freibourg family exchanges hugs as best it can. Leonard fixes his father with an intent, cross-eyed look that his mother recognizes.

"No no," she says sharply. "Put it down."

He puts his father down. Then, musing, he picks up a

police sergeant, studies him and puts his head in his mouth. Because Leonard has very few teeth, the sergeant emerges physically unharmed, but flushed and jabbering with fear.

"Put it *down*," says Mrs. Freibourg. Then, to the lieutenant: "You'd better get him something to eat. And you'd better find some way for me to change him," she adds, referring obliquely to the appalling stench. The sergeant looks puzzled until she points out a soiled mass clinging to the big toe of the left foot. "His diaper is a mess." She turns to her husband. "You didn't even change him. And what did you do to him while my back was turned?"

"The beta culture," Dr. Freibourg says miserably. He is pale and shaken. "It works."

"Well you'd better find some way to reverse it," Mrs. Freibourg says. "And you'd better do it soon."

"Of course my dear," Dr. Freibourg says, with more confidence than he actually feels. He steps into the police car waiting to rush him to the laboratory. "I'll stay up all night if I have to."

The mother looks at Leonard appraisingly. "You may have to stay up all week."

Meanwhile, the semi filled with unwrapped Wonder Bread and the tank truck have arrived with Leonard's dinner. His diaper has been arranged by one of the Cherokee crews that helped build the Verrazano Narrows bridge, with preliminary cleansing done by hoses trained on him by the Auxiliary Fire Department. Officials at Madison Square Garden have loaned a tarpaulin to cover Leonard in his hastily constructed crib of hoardings, and graffitists are at work on the outsides. "Paint a duck," Mrs. Freibourg says to one of the minority groups with spray cans, "I want him to be happy here." Leonard cuddles the life-sized Steiff rhinoceros loaned by FAO Schwartz, and goes to sleep.

His mother stands vigil until almost midnight, in case Leonard cries in the night, and across town, in his secret laboratory, Dr. Freibourg has assembled some of the best brains in contemporary science to help him in his search for the antidote.

Meanwhile, all the major television networks have established prime-time coverage, with camera crews remaining on the site to record late developments.

At the mother's insistence, riot-trained police have been withdrawn to the vicinity of the Plaza. The mood in the park is one of quiet confidence. Despite the lights and the magnified sound of heavy breathing, fatigue seizes Mrs. Freibourg and, some time near dawn, she sleeps.

5 a.m. Sunday, Sept. 17: Unfortunately, like most babies, Leonard is an early riser. Secure in a mother's love, he wakes up early and sneaks out of his crib, heading across 79th Street and out of the park, making for the river. Although the people at the site are roused by the creak as he levels the hoardings and the crash of a trailer accidentally toppled and then carefully righted, it is too late to head him off. He has escaped the park in the nick of time, because he has grown in the night, and there is some question as to whether he would have fit between the buildings on East 79th Street in another few hours.

5:10 a.m.: Leonard mashes a portion of the East River Drive on the way into the water. Picking up a taxi, he runs it back and forth on the remaining portion of the road, going, "Rmmmm, Rmmmmm, RMRMMM-MM."

5:11 a.m.: Leonard's mother arrives. She is unable to attract his attention because he has put down the taxi and is splashing his hands in the water, swamping boats for several miles on either side of him.

Across town, Dr. Freibourg has succeeded in shrinking a cat to half-size but he can't find any way to multiply the dosage without emptying laboratories all over the nation to make enough of the salient ingredient. He is frantic because he knows there isn't time.

5:15: In the absence of any other way to manage the problem, fire hoses are squirting milk at Leonard, hit-or-miss. He is enraged by the misses and starts throwing his toys.

The National Guard, summoned when Leonard started down 79th Street to the river, attempts to deter the infant with light artillery.

Naturally the baby starts to cry.

5:30 a.m.: Despite his mother's best efforts to silence him with bullhorn and Steiff rhinoceros proffered at the end of a giant crane, Leonard is still bellowing.

The Joint Chiefs of Staff arrive, and attempt to survey the problem. Leonard has more or less filled the river at the point where he is sitting. His tears have raised the water level, threatening to inundate portions of the FDR Drive. Speaker trucks simultaneously broadcasting recordings of "Chitty-Chitty Bang Bang" have reduced his bellows to sobs, so the immediate threat of buildings collapsing from the vibrations has been minimized, but there is still the problem of shipping, as he plays boat with tugs and barges but, because of his age, is bored easily, and has thrown several toys into the harbor, causing shipping disasters along the entire Eastern Seaboard. Now he is lifting the top off a building and has begun to examine its contents, picking out the parts that look good to eat and swallowing them whole. After an abbreviated debate, the Joint Chiefs discuss the feasibility of nuclear weaponry of the limited type. They have ruled out tranquilizer cannon because of the size of the problem, and there is some question as to whether massive doses of poison would have any effect.

Overhearing some of the top-level planning, the distraught mother has seized Channel Five's recording equipment to make a nationwide appeal. Now militant mothers from all the boroughs are marching on the site, threatening massive retaliation if the baby is harmed in any way.

Pollution problems are becoming acute.

The UN is meeting around the clock.

The premiers of all the major nations have sent messages of concern with guarded offers of help.

6:30 a.m.: Leonard has picked the last good bits from his building and now he has tired of playing fire truck and he is bored. Just as the tanks rumble down East 79th Street, levelling their cannon, and the SAC bombers take off from their secret base, the baby plops on his hands and starts hitching out to sea.

6:34: The baby has reached deep water now. SAC planes report that Leonard, made buoyant by the enormous quantities of fat he carries, is floating happily; he has made his breakfast on a whale.

Dr. Freibourg arrives. "Substitute ingredients. I've found the antidote."

Dilys Freibourg says, "Too little and too late."

"But our baby."

"He's not our baby any more. He belongs to the ages now."

The Joint Chiefs are discussing alternatives. "I wonder if we should look for him."

Mrs. Freibourg says, "I wouldn't if I were you."

The Supreme Commander looks from mother to Joint Chiefs. "Oh well, he's already in international waters."

The Joint Chiefs exchange looks of relief. "Then it's not our problem."

Suffused by guilt, Dr. Freibourg looks out to sea. "I wonder what will become of him."

His wife says, "Wherever he goes, my heart will go with him, but I wonder if all that salt water will be good for his skin."

COMING SOON: THE ATTACK OF THE GIANT TODDLER

The Wandering Gentile

Hath not a Gentile eyes? Hath not a Gentile hands, organs, dimensions, senses, affections, passions. . . . If you prick us do we not bleed?

Perhaps you haven't heard of me. Oh everybody's heard of him, the Jew who offended the Saviour on the day of the Crucifixion, and was doomed to wander. He gets written about and sung about, there are dozens of legends and at least two novels that I know of, but not one of them so much as mentions me: the Wandering Gentile. I guess I was standing too close to him the day it happened; it's the classic case of your innocent bystander, I've been around just as long as he has and it's me who takes care of the day-to-day matters, when we're going to eat next, where we're going to stay, what we're going to use for money.

Not all Jews are practical about money, no matter what you've been brought up to think. All Bright Eyes cares about is his image, and I'm the one who has to get the job in the next city we come to while he sits around and bemoans our fate. Maybe that's one reason I have a better grip on things; I guess it's what you could call the Protestant work ethic: no time to sit around and bemoan our fate. Of course he has a reputation as a great thinker, who wouldn't, with all that time on his hands? So would I, if I wasn't working every living minute.

Well let me tell you, he wasn't thinking the day it happened. I suppose I wasn't either, it took me a good hundred years to figure out what was going on, but how was I supposed to know? Believe me, if I'd had any idea what was happening I would have done the Right Thing right then and there: given the prisoner a drink, begged Him to rest, helped in any way I could. Here's what I would not have done: under no circumstances would I have yelled Faster, which is what our immortal friend apparently did.

Of course he denies it, but it was all so long ago that we're both fuzzy about the details. When I get laid off or we manage to hitch a ride to the next place, we sit around and try to put it together, but to tell the truth I never did know exactly what happened, and if he knew he is, according to the one shrink I consulted, blocking it. Either that or he is scared to death I will find out the real truth and try to kill him.

I do know I was on the execution route that day, and I saw the party pass. And Bright Eyes, my friend the Jew, was either the cobbler who fixed my sandal before I reported to work that day, in which case his name is Ahasuerus, or he was Kartaphilus, the other guard in the doorway at Pilate's, where I worked. I know perfectly well I was in both places but that jerk won't admit to either, and he says he isn't the hostler who refused the victim a drink, either, although he and I did go through our Huntsman phase a couple of hundred years ago, tooling around in the forest uttering ghastly cries. The reports vary too: either he really did yell Faster, or else he said, You can't rest here, or else he said, Drink from that Camel's footprint if You're thirsty, all of them things only a damn fool would have done. In any case the riposte is clearly reported; the Victim fixed him with His eyes and said, "You will tarry until I come again." Well tarry he did, but whenever it happened, I must have been standing too close because I got some of it, or maybe it was that they needed somebody to stay around to make good and sure he did tarry; it was the damndest thing: I tarried too.

Who knew? I can report that by the time I met up with him again he had already changed his name and no he does not have a red cross burned into his forehead, although he does have a funny stain that shows up in certain lights, and I would also have to report that when he is left to his own devices he is something of a whiner, which is what he was doing when I bumped into him again, in what I guess we would have to call A.D. 133.

By that time I had buried my family. When I say my family I mean my whole family: wife, children, grandchildren, the works. The day of the execution we heard there was a Jew who had been cursed, and although I converted to Christianity within the year, I never gave the story another thought. I certainly never connected it with the fact that I was still young and springy while all about me were losing theirs; I attributed that to clean living, and told the grandchildren they ought to eat better, and get more exercise. They were getting wrinkled and desiccated: it was enough to make you sick: I would have taken off after the wife died if it hadn't been for my sense of responsibility. As it was I stayed to bury the last one—why did he fix me with a look of such resentment when he died? He wasn't the only one; the town rose up against me with pikes and staffs, they claimed I was a demon, but it was sheer jealousy. Well I can tell you, being immortal is no picnic either. But I promised not to whine.

They chased me into the desert, where the sun was so

fierce that even the most vicious of them gave up the chase. I thought I was going to die. Fat chance! Some months later I fetched up against a mountain with a lean-to on the side of it; I climbed up and there he was.

It was the damndest thing; we recognized each other. I said, "Haven't I seen you somewhere before?"

He staggered back a step or two and threw his hand over his brow because he has always liked melodrama, saying, "You."

"What do you mean, You?"

He looked a fright. His hair was flying and his eyes burned, and even though he pretended to be distracted and raving and always claims he does not remember the fateful day, he said, "You were there that day, when I offended Him."

No use pretending I didn't understand. "Yes, I was around."

Then he fixed me with those glittering eyes and said, "Well, don't you think that's a little strange?"

"What's strange?"

"You still being around." He leaned forward, and just in case I wasn't ready to face facts, he parted his hair to show me that stain on his forehead, and hissed, "Everybody else has been dead for years."

"That's all very well," I said, "but I take care of myself, I exercise . . ."

"You idiot. I thought I was the only one."

"The only . . ."

"But now you."

I saw my reflection glinting in his eyes and I understood how old he was, how old we were going to get. "You don't mean . . ."

"Exactly." He pulled his rags around him and opened his mouth in what I would soon recognize as one of his lamentations; he was in full cry in a matter of seconds, and it was hours before I could get him to quiet down. I still don't know whether he wails for the joy of it or whether it is one of the terms of his condemnation, but I do know one thing, and I will never forget it: right before he threw his head back he looked me dead in the eye and said, "Why couldn't you have been a girl?"

It was awful. I suppose it was because it was the first time, but I can tell you it is absolutely awful to watch somebody keen; first they rant and then they moan and then they wallow, with exhibitionistic rag-rending and breast-beating and never mind the sensibilities of whoever happens to be around. Jeremiah could not have done it better, and even I would have to admit that my wandering partner has style. On the other hand it was hot work waiting around for him to pull himself together; what's more he began to repeat himself and I found it downright annoying to watch him carrying on like that. You'd think he was the only one in the world with problems, when there I was in the same boat, and new to the business at that. I was disgusted by the condition of his rags, how filthy the hut was, what his hair looked like, all matted with blood because he *will* pull it out by the roots, and so while he wallowed I busied myself about the hut, putting things to rights. I started a stew and did the wash and when I had run out of things to do and he was still at it I stood over him and said, "That's enough."

There was foam on his lips. "Wanderer, the curs-éd wanderer."

So I gave him a little kick. "I said, that's enough."

He opened one eye. "What did you say?"

I helped him up. "I said, you might as well make the best of it."

He brightened considerably when he saw how neat the place was, that he had a clean change of rags and a hot dinner for once, instead of those wretched roots and berries. "You're very kind."

So I took him in hand. "Look old man, nobody has to live like this."

"I thought it was appropriate."

"For thousands of years?"

"Don't think thousands," he said, "it's too depressing."

I said, "Stiff upper lip, old thing. It's always well to prepare for the worst."

He wasn't listening. He was feeling around in the sand. "My prayer shawl, you forgot to wash my prayer shawl."

I was so busy helping him pull himself together that I didn't even hear what I was saying: "I'm sorry, I forgot, I'll catch it next time I do the washing."

The next thing I knew he was hurtling past me, headed for the cliff; I hurled myself after him and caught him by the ankles just as he went over.

"Let go," he said, "I have nothing to live for."

I hauled him back up. "We have each other."

Right, a rotten basis for a relationship.

And at the time, I didn't even know about the women. He had this thing about, what was it, unendurable pleasure indefinitely prolonged, not that he believed in it, but that the quest gave him something to live for. If I'd had any idea how many times I would stand guard outside some silken doorway, waiting while he took his pleasure, fencing with irate husbands and outraged fathers, I would have let him go off that cliff. But if I had, what good would it have done me? I would have heard him moaning on the rocks below, because we get hurt but we never die, and sooner or later I would have had to go down to apply bandages and haul him up.

I won't bore you with the details of the last two thousand years. Think of us in a montage of funny costumes, wearing different hats. Try to conceive of the number of times I got fed up and left for absolutely the last time, the number of tearful reunions because in the end everybody else always dies and only he and I are left. Consider the variety of scenes we have played in bistros and brothels and on park benches from Cathay to Chicago and perhaps you will also catch the cacaphony of insults exchanged in a thousand different settings, in a dozen different languages. Legends spring up in our footsteps like toadstools, but in case you want to know we probably were Dante and Virgil, or maybe it was Heloïse and Abelard, exchanging letters to while away a boring dozen years, all right, maybe he always did write better than I do, but it's only lately he's begun to rub it in; we were also Quixote and Sancho Panza or was it Roland and Oliver, and I can report there is something to the rumor that we were Boswell and Johnson when that thing was at its most popular, but I won't say which of us was which. Early on we went through a gladiator period, followed by a samurai period; we did a certain amount of whistling in mountain passes and menaced travellers on the Bosphorus for an entire season, and we definitely did a stint in Argentina; I had to pretend to be the Nazi, luring survivors of the Third Reich back to our place so he could conduct the war trials, except he kept getting distracted and lamenting instead, so I had to do the rest. In bad times for Jews I used to masquerade as the master with him the servant under my protection, and in good times the roles would be reversed. Picture us on a merry-go-round, our two horses rising and falling in alternation; the hats and costumes change every time one of us goes up or the other down and only the theme is constant; he laments and prays and I clean up, and if I complain he reminds me of Mary and Martha, and says after all, imagine the jobs I have held, the love affairs I have thwarted for the sake of long-dead maidens, the assorted lynchings and *autos da fé* I have averted, the ingenious attempts at suicide.

But why am I reliving all this, or should I say, why now? I suppose it is because we went along in most of the same ways for so many centuries that I always assumed certain things were constant, but in the last few decades things have shifted, and I would have to say the whole picture is changing, and for my money, for the worse. What's more, I do not like his attitude.

Of course it was always there, but I didn't have to face up to it until fairly recently. I'm afraid it was Freud. No sooner did we hear about all that than we had to nip off to Vienna so Bright Eyes could throw himself upon the couch. "After all," he said, "who is more complex, richer in material, face it, who has more interesting problems?" I shot him a look that should have embarrassed him but he was deep in his notes for the next day's session; yes, Dr. Freud, he wrote his lines before he even got to you, and if you thought the patient was subject to a particularly interesting delusion, I have news. Meanwhile, as they say in the books, he was becoming impossible to live with. He always came home from those sessions with a self-important grin and if I complained because he was late or mentioned in passing that working in the *wurst* works was no picnic, he'd say, "Classic. Absolutely classic." We were paying through the nose for that bit of self-indulgence, but when I would try to find out what went on in those sessions, to get our money's worth, he would only give me one of his superior looks and say, "You couldn't hope to understand."

So there was that, and once he got the habit he couldn't kick it. I've kept him in analysts ever since. Then there were the 1930s, when I sold apples and worked on the TVA project while he read literature, and the next thing I knew I was working in a war plant to put him through graduate school, Columbia, if you can imagine. Don't ask about transcripts, scores; when you've been around as long as we have you become adept at providing the proper papers for anything you want to undertake. I must say it took him years to get that doctorate, years and years, but in 1950 he came home and said, "OK, old friend, it's time for you to rest, I'm going to support us now." I said, "What if I don't *want* to rest," but damned if he hadn't already accepted a job teaching English at Bennington. He looked so smug I wanted to hit him. "Relax. It's high time you took it easy."

Well you can tell a Protestant to take it easy but getting him to do it is another thing. I hated it in the country, I fretted, I stewed, I became a gentleman farmer while Bright Eyes alternately beat his breast and chased the undergraduates and every woman on the junior faculty. If it hadn't been for that imbroglio with the instructor's wife, we would be there still. As it was we moved on to CCNY, but it became apparent that after all those centuries on the road, Bright Eyes was beginning to settle. I would have to admit that I was the one who got us down to Argentina to hunt Nazis, by then I was wild from the inactivity, and it was me who insisted we climb the Matterhorn the year he got his Guggenheim. Up until this century we had gone along together more or less shoulder to shoulder, I had thought of us as equals, but then he got the appointment to Columbia (I am withholding his present name, which you would recognize at once), and about the same time he started running around with the gang from the New York Review of Books, and his chauvinism surfaced. I never got to go to the literary cocktail parties in his honor, even when I was invited; when he lectured at Princeton I had to stay home, and when he received the National Book Award for his critical work: *Literature, a Long View*, I didn't even get to hear his speech. Let's face it, he was getting uppity. Worse, he was ashamed of me.

It all came to a head when he got home from the National Book Awards; he was already busy with his note pad, cataloguing slights so he could recite them to his analyst. I don't remember precisely what was said but I remember me getting madder and madder, saying, "Your analyst, your analyst, why can't I have an analyst?"

He was on me in a flash: "You don't have enough problems."

"Just because I've never been a whiner, like some people..."

He was cranking up to keen: "What do you know about real problems?"

Well it was more than I could take. "I've been around just as long as you have."

Then it came out, the real truth, what has always stood between us. "Yeah, but you're only a WASP."

It was then that I knew I had to kill him.

Naturally it wasn't going to be easy, but I had, let's say, a little more insight into the problem than your average murderer; I knew that guns and knives were out, pills and poison a mere bagatelle in the face of immortality, and it wasn't going to do any earthly good to arrange a mugging or have him run over by a truck. In addition to everything else our recuperative powers are extraordinary; in our brief experience in the Tenth Crusade, great gaping bloody wounds would heal themselves overnight. I thought about tying a washing machine to his feet and throwing the whole arrangement off the Brooklyn Bridge but I knew better; he would wait down there until the ropes rotted and then float up to confront me with a series of reproaches and an incredibly boring disquistion on the nature of being buried full fathom five. It was going to have to be immolation and dismemberment. The small bits could go into the Dispos-all and everything ungrindable would have to be wrapped and mailed to as many foreign ports as it took. If I couldn't dispose of him completely I could at least disperse him so thoroughly that millennia would pass before he could pull himself together to reproach me, and who knew, by that time, maybe WASPS would be in the ascendency.

He came home early of course, after I had obtained the blowtorch but before I had a chance to drug the Martinis or soak the place with gasoline, and so all I could do when he confronted me was level the blowtorch at his belly, saying, "Okay, baby, this is it."

He said, "That's all very well, friend, but if I die you die with me."

I remember yelling, "And cheap at the price."

Then I let the blue flame lick his belly and his clothes caught and his flesh had just begun to crackle when I felt a pain in my own midsection, so excruciating that I had to drop the torch.

"Don't stop," he cried. "Not now, when we're so close."

I was clawing at my belly, gasping with pain. Was that really smoke rising from me? Did I smell my own burning flesh or does it turn out I have more problems than I thought? "I can't."

"Come on." Good Lord, he was begging me. "Come on, come *on*."

"I can't."

He straightened, grimacing because he knew how quickly he would mend. "I should have known I couldn't count on you to do it right."

"You mean you wanted this?"

He was really cross. "Why else would I let you hang around?"

"All right, smarty, what made you so sure I would do it?"

"It always happens if we hang around you guys for long enough." His martyred smile was more than I could take. "Sooner or later it always happens, all we have to do is wait."

"That's a rotten thing to say. Look at everything I did for you." I wanted to hit him. "Besides, it isn't true."

Well that was what he was waiting for. "Who masterminded that execution you and I were at? It wasn't the Jews, baby." God, he was smug. "Who drove in the nails?"

"That does it." I picked up the blowtorch and threw it at him. "We're through."

But he had already put on a raincoat to cover the

burned spot and now he was stuffing books and underwear into an attaché case. He was *packing*.

I didn't want to ask but I couldn't help it, I said, "Where are you going?"

"Israel." He was in the doorway by that time. "Are you coming?"

. . . .

All right, all *right*.

Moon

For reasons which only the missing generation knew, nobody could find the children of the hippies. There had to be hundreds of thousands, because hundreds of thousands of them had been born around the tag-end of the '60s and in the first dreggy years of the '70s, but nobody knew where they were. Most of them didn't show up on any of the records because they had tumbled into life in lofts and broken-down farmhouses and culverts along the major roadways, growing up like puppies in what their parents fondly called freedom, if they thought about it at all. They all had names like Moon or Star or Shimmer or Nahome, Barkas or even God because after all they were the New People, without, what was it, without hangups, and they were going to be completely different. These children of peace and love were supposed to change the world, except they hadn't. Instead they seemed to have disappeared into the earth like rainwater without changing much of anything, and when people from the old days, like parents or litter-mates, went looking for them, they were almost impossible to find.

If Moon No-Name Rainwater was hard to find it was because he wanted to be hard to find, he didn't want to see Gretchen X or any of the others because they threatened him with bad memories. From the moment he had taken control of his own life, it had been blissfully square. He had a square wife from a New England family and one square kid and he worked for Aetna in Hartford now, a computer programmer. After work he went home to a split-level ranch in a housing tract which he had bought into under the name Ralph Adams Bissell, and his true family history bore little relation to the family history he related to little Ralph Adams Bissell III, whom he called Biff and with whom he tossed the ball around on Saturdays like any other suburban Dad.

The boy, Biff, grew up under the impression that his Dad's early life had been more or less like his own, give or take the two-way television and the seven hours of homework and the intercity hovercraft. He had no idea that the funny redheaded lady who spoke to him in the supermarket was really Gretchen X, his own true grandmother; he did know that his father took one look at her and bolted, dumping all their packages at the checkout screen before the scanner could come up with a total.

On the street, Biff thought he heard her calling after them. "Moon, Moon baby, it's me. Don't you know me, Moon?"

Despite his father's haste he dragged his feet because he had liked her right away. She had on dungarees and an old shirt, things a kid would wear, and she stood with her feet planted wide in basketball shoes and talked to him just like another kid. He couldn't understand why his father's face was grey and uncompromising now, or why he wouldn't say anything, or why his fingers were trembling on the wheel.

"She was only being friendly," he said at last.

"You're old enough to know better. God only knows what she had in mind."

"Should we go back for the groceries?" Biff noted with alarm that his father's upper lip was greasy with sweat. "Are you all right?"

"You can't be too careful," his father said, looking back to be sure they weren't being followed. "You can't trust anyone." His face relaxed as he nosed the car into the iris of the garage, safely home.

She was on the corner the next day when Biff came home from school. "Hi, kid."

She acted so much like a kid his age that he couldn't keep from grinning. "Hi."

"Did the old man tell you about me?"

"He's scared of you. He thinks you want to sell me off, or worse." His books were getting heavy so he shifted them to his other hip.

"Are those books all yours?"

He grimaced. "Homework."

"Dump them and let's talk."

He poked them at the garage and the iris opened to receive them. He felt pounds lighter. His hands lifted, almost floating.

"Right on," Gretchen said. "Where can we talk?"

The tract ended at the lip of a wooded ravine, where children weren't supposed to go. Biff liked it because he could sit on a rock within earshot of home and pretend to be alone.

"My name is Gretchen," Gretchen said when they were planted on opposite ends of a log. "Look, I'm your grandmother."

"My grandmothers live in Hartford."

"Is that what he told you?"

"So how could you be my grandmother?"

"They stole him when he was a little kid," Gretchen said. "We were free as air, happy as pigs, and the state took him away from me."

"That's terrible."

"And now he has this ticky-tacky life in that ticky-tacky house and you're all happily forever after, right?"

Biff had never thought about it. "I guess so."

Gretchen stood. "So I guess I'll buzz off now, you're all happy and I'm just in the way."

"Wait a minute, who said you're in the way?"

"I could see the way he looked at me, and your mother, if she knew she'd have hysterics." She was watching him carefully. "People like them are afraid of people like us."

"Are you a hippie?"

"You might call it that." She was standing with her hands thrust in the pockets of her dungarees and her head back, and in spite of all the wrinkles, and the fact that the red hair was probably dyed, she didn't look like a grown-up lady to him; she looked ready for anything, young. "So if things are cool here I guess I'll split."

"I thought there weren't any left."

She grinned ruefully. "We kind of went out of style."

He was looking hard at her now, trying to figure out what it was he liked so much. Partly it was the way she talked, not grown-up to child, do this, do that, like his mother, but eye-to-eye, as if they could both be her age or they could both be ten. "I thought they all freaked out and died."

"That's what they want you to think." She squatted, her eyes crackling. "Let me tell you what it's like."

She said a long time ago her life was ticky-tacky, just like his, until she split; she talked a lot about the, what was it, military industrial complex, and she said uptight a lot, everybody back home was uptight so she cut out to someplace she called the Haight. She did dope for a while, she said, she was all strung out and after a while she met Lance, that might be Biff's grandfather, he was a bass player, and when she found out she was going to have a baby she split for Oregon, she landed on a farm with a bunch of other kids, they worked it for this old lady, who, when she died, willed it to them and they lived there to this day. It was beautiful on the farm, Gretch got herself all cleaned out, no more dope, no more, and she had the kid and they used to sit on the porch and watch the sun go down and other times they would run around naked in the deep green woods and she loved that kid, lord how she loved him, they were like the sun and the moon and that's why she called him Moon.

"You mean my father's name is Moon?" Biff could already hear himself coming back at his father, when he got on him about his marks, or cleaning his room like a normal person instead of living in a welter of dirty clothes; he would draw himself up and look his father in the eye, saying: Look here, Moon.

She was saying, "You would have loved it out there, Moon."

He said, gently, "I'm not him, Grandma, I'm Biff."

"You'd better call me Gretch." She stood again, hanging her thumbs on her back pockets. "I know you're not Moon. Look, kid, who would you like to be?"

Without thinking it out Biff said, "Archer."

"Archer," she said, learning it. "Right."

His watch had begun to ping: Mom was home. "Look, Gretch, I've got all this homework, can, uh, can you come back tomorrow?"

"You really want me to?"

"Gretch, you're my grandmother."

"Right." She punched him on the arm. "Right right. Look, I think these were your grandfather's, if that was your grandfather." She gave him a string of beautiful blue beads.

Through the next week he had the good sense to keep the beads hidden until everybody else was in bed and he could conclude they were asleep. Then he would go into the bathroom and turn them over in his fingers, looking at the little chips of silver and the azure veins that ran through them and thinking about a place in which you sat on the front porch and ran in the woods without having to do anything you didn't want to do, and at supper he would look at Ralph (Moon) Adams Bissell, his father, and wonder what had crazed him to the point where he wanted to sit at the head of a tiny table where the same things were said over the same kinds of food every single night. In the afternoons he sat in the ravine and talked with Gretchen, who told him about her love for Deke and her love for Francis and her lifelong love for Man Superstar, her own true mate, how they ran together and loved together for all their days and how they lived together even now in a place where there weren't any clocks and there were never any rules.

Biff started having trouble with his family: he would be dreaming at his desk and his mother would come and watch him not doing his homework. When she couldn't stand it another minute she would say, "Biff, what's the matter with you?"

"Nothing, Mom, I'm fine."

"Your class standing, Biff. Your work. You want to go to college, don't you?"

"Sure, Mom. Sure." Feeling the beads in his pocket he would wonder did he want to, really?

"Then you'd better put your mind on your work, or you'll end up just like . . ."

Just like your father. Just another computer programmer in the mill. At the back of Biff's mind was a green wood with naked figures running: Gretchen and the strong-browed Man Superstar with their bright hair streaming. Gretchen said they harvested the vegetables together, men, women, kids all naked to the waist and all like new; they would lie with their ears to the earth, spread out between the bean rows, listening to things grow. What was the matter with his father, living in this ticky-tacky neighborhood when he could be back there in Oregon, sitting on the porch? They could all be out there in Oregon, looking at the woods and smelling the uncut hay, just waiting for the sun to go down.

"I was with Man Superstar by that time, I don't know what we did wrong or how they found out about it, but the people came out from town and said I had to send Moon No-Name Rainwater, my child that was going to grow up free from hangups, I was supposed to put clothes on him and sent him in town to school. Well we fought that one for as long as we could and finally we had to send him, his poor belly strangled by a belt and his feet all squinched in his first pair of shoes, I should have known better," she said darkly. "From that day on he was altered, the system got him and it changed him, the system got him in its clutches that first day of school."

Biff stroked her knee because there were tears coursing down her cheeks now, he said, "Take it easy, Gretch," adding a phrase he had picked up from her. "Be cool."

"Right." She snuffed it back up. "Honey, you're right. You'd better run along now, or his wife will be on your back, you know, about being late?" She meant Biff's mother but she couldn't bring herself to say it.

"Okay, Gretch."

His mother was at the door, menacing. "All right, where were you?"

"I just went to talk to a kid for a minute."

"You have homework, Biff, you can't afford to talk to kids."

"It was only for a minute."

"All right," she said, pushing him into the house. "Don't get into college, see if I care. You can always drive a garbage truck."

"It's only fifth grade, Mom."

"Watch your mouth."

That night his father took up the case. "What's gotten into you?"

"Nothing, Dad," Biff said, looking into his father's face for traces of that lost, naked child Gretchen told him about: where are you, Moon?

"You're behind in your work." Ralph (Moon) Adams went on gravely. "I've had a phone call from the school."

"The school?" Biff remembered how the people took Moon away and turned him into this ordinary man. "Who cares about the school?"

"Son, it's the key to your future."

"Oh, Man, it sucks you into the system. That's all about school."

Ralph's head snapped around; he fixed the boy with his eyes and would not let him look away. "Who have you been talking to?"

The beads were cool against the boy's fingertips. "Nobody, man."

Biff already knew he had gone too far. His father was waiting for him the next afternoon, and his father drove him home from school and marched him to his desk and stood there, waiting for him to start to work. The boy looked up. "Look, can I go to Jimmy's for a minute? I forgot a book."

"No."

"Then I won't be able to do my geography," he said, because it always worked.

"But you'll get behind." Ralph knew he was beaten. "OK, go and get the book."

Gretchen was waiting in the ravine, and when he finished talking she said, "You know, you don't have to go back."

"They're my parents, Gretch."

"Have it your way, but let me tell you something first." She squatted, rocking back and forth, and told him about the last time she saw Moon, how the authorities came and took him away for good when he was only eight; they pulled him out of her arms and when Man Superstar tried to stop them it took eight of them to hold him down, and when they couldn't hold him they drew guns on the family, yes, she said, family, but better than any other kind of family because they weren't born to each other, they were together because they wanted to be. They took Moon away from her, they said it was for his own good, and now he wasn't her Moon any more, he had changed, he would never be happy or free again because they pulled him into the system and he changed.

The story took longer than they thought; by the time Gretchen finished they were both crying, Biff hugged her and she rocked him while they cried some more and he promised not to change. It took him a while to get his face back to normal and when he came back to the house he had forgotten the geography book so his father had to spank him and lock him in his room. Sulking at his desk, he was aware of the key turning in the lock and his father peeking in to be sure he was working. The cool presence of the beads at the bottom of his pocket did not so much console as remind him: there was more somewhere, and it was better. There had to be more.

Which meant that after school the next day he sneaked out through the gym because he knew his father would be waiting. He might even know about Gretchen and try to tell on him. He darted around the building and crossed the street behind his father's car, murmuring, with a quick gesture, "See ya later, Moon."

Gretchen was waiting at the ravine. As if she already knew, she lifted a backpack and bedroll. "Come on, kid. Let's split."

They came out on the far side of the ravine. Gretchen found an unlocked car and with practiced fingers jumped the wires and started the motor. Within a matter of minutes they were on the highway, heading west. Biff's heart was jangling with a dozen different messages and because he couldn't shake the picture of his parents' faces when they found out he was gone he made up a little tune and whistled it through his teeth, adding words as they crossed the state line: Freedom now, freedom now, freedom NOW.

They ate at fast food places and slept on the ground and half the time they ran in cars and half the time they hitched. Finally they turned off a highway in Oregon, going from a paved road onto a bumpy two-track drive through a green woods that was just as Gretch described it, pulling up at last in front of a ramshackle farmhouse with people lying around on the porch. To Biff's surprise, nobody seemed to notice much, except to move slightly so he and Gretch could pick their way through to the front door. "Home, son," she said, stopping to stretch and breathe in the fresh air, the familiar smells. "We're home."

The first thing was, it was dark inside and it smelled worse than Biff could have imagined, a mixture of old cooking and dirty clothes and animal hair and a couple of other things he didn't recognize. There seemed to be heaps everywhere: heaps of cloth and bedding and splintered wood, heaps of books and rusting things, heaps of bodies, limp groups that flexed slightly and tossed on the mounds which were either bed or clothing; there was no way to be sure. The second thing was that he couldn't recognize any of the people she had told him about: Deke and Marva and Sissy and Anne Twelvetrees and all the wonderful kids who ran naked in the woods and worked the garden stripped to the waist in warm weather, so that after they had picked their way to the stairs Biff stopped and dug his feet in, saying, "Wait."

Maybe because it came out sharper than he had intended, she turned quickly, saying, "What's the matter, honey?"

He was scared to death he was going to cry and so he said, too loud, "Where is everybody?"

She seemed puzzled, anxious. "Like who?"

"Man. Man Superstar for one."

"Oh, Man." Her face relaxed. "Let's go see him, he's out back."

There he was, asleep on the back porch with his coon dog curled up next to him and his hat over his face; he was as big and hard-muscled as advertised, so far he looked *right*, but when Gretchen stuck her toe into his bicep and he sat up, Biff had to keep himself from running off to cry because Man Superstar might have been beautiful once but now he was only an old guy. A lot of his back teeth were missing and his face was seamed and collapsing into itself like an old bed pillow; if he was glad to see Gretchen he didn't show it much, he only said, "Oh, yeah, hey Gretch," and then, not exactly thrilled, "Who's the kid?"

"Moon's boy," she said, adding, to Biff's surprise, "Moon's boy Archer."

"Archer?" Biff had almost forgotten. "My mother calls me . . . Oh yeah, Archer. Yeah."

Man Superstar pulled his hat back over his face. "Yeah, yeah man."

Then Gretchen led the boy upstairs, past a mess of rabbits in a cage ("Marva's pets") and a dog wearing a diaper ("In heat. She's in heat half the time") and three old ladies in dungarees who hummed to themselves on a broken down sofa in the upstairs hall ("Remember Galen and the Pipe Dreams? These are the original Pipe Dreams"), through what appeared to be a bedroom ("Man and I crash here") and into a tiny closet with a high window, and she pointed to a rumpled sleeping bag that had been used to wrap something sticky and a carton half full of nameless untouchables made out of cloth, and said, "Make yourself to home, Moon honey, everything I have is yours."

Biff pulled the raggedy flowered curtain between the closet and the main room and stuffed his face against his knees so Gretchen wouldn't hear him cry. Then he thought maybe dinner would make him feel better about everything and so he went downstairs. They had thrown together a stew in his honor and for tonight, at least, Gretch said they would all eat at the same time. He knew he was supposed to be flattered but he was bothered by the dirt on the table and on the floor around the table and on some of the things they were eating out of and Marva and one of The Pipe Dreams started a long wrangle about who was going to wash the dishes after this gig and Biff asked to be excused.

"You don't have to ask, Archer, baby," Gretchen said. "You're one of us now, and you can do anything you want."

They were all sitting or crouching around the table in various attitudes of indifference or gluttony; Marva mumbled something about the munchies as she snagged the leftover chunks of gristle on Biff's plate and he fled the scene, thinking: At least she didn't call me Moon.

The next day was better. He got used to the crawly feeling the used sleeping bag gave him and when he got up the next morning Gretchen gave him a hard roll and sat down with him on the floor by the dilapidated dresser, pulling out one after another in her collection of beads. Some of them were chipped, cheap and ugly, and some were pretty in the way stones you find on the beach are pretty and some of them were beautiful: opals on one string, three strings of rose quartz, one amber set, one jade. Sitting on the floor next to her, Biff could look into the sparkling piles and recall some of the longing he had felt listening to her back in the ravine. Later she took him into town—right at the bottom of the hill as the crow flies, but longer by the road. Lunching at a Supermac, gobbling burgers as fast as they came down the chute, he could remember the excitement he had felt munching burgers in Buffalo, Chicago, as far west as Abilene. They went into the drug store together and she bought him a Cocola, a month's allowance shot right there, he thought, but she was happy to be doing the town with him and she didn't care about expense. She faked a chargecard with something she found in a garbage can and got them both into the movies, which they stayed through twice, and when they rolled into the farmhouse late that night Biff was almost happy; if it hadn't been for the complicated noises all those other people made, sleeping, and the one smell he couldn't identify, he might have slept just fine.

As it was, he rolled a lot, hurting his elbows on the floor, and the more he thought about it the more he thought there was something missing, and when he tried to figure out what that could be the only thing he could hit on was his bed lamp with the night light in the base and his favorite pillow, but he cried as if there were a lot more things than that, and when he couldn't cry any more he slid off into a sleep that was never solid enough to be called that; it was more of an uncomfortable doze.

The next morning he was in the kitchen early waiting for breakfast, but nobody ever fixed breakfast or any other meal so far as he could tell; instead they shambled in and out when they felt like it, eating peanut butter out of the jar with twice-licked fingers or taking a box of cereal to a corner to eat, spilling it on the floor. "This way nobody has to worry about dishes," Marva explained, throwing him a box of Cocoa Puffs, oblivious of the ones which had escaped and slid around underfoot. Everybody was pretty old so that Biff had to conclude their eyes were bad and they just couldn't *see* the mess, the dried puddles on the threadbare rugs and the food smears on the walls. The smell, or at least the part he hadn't recognized, came from the gravity toilet: something about wastes transforming into compost as they went down a chute, except something had misfired, if that was the right word, some months back, and now it was all backed up in the chute, so that after his third night in the little closet, listening to people fight and snore and cry out in the dark, Biff had asked, tactfully, whether he could try sleeping on the roof. Except for the bugs, that was better. He looked up at the dark trees, which were as Gretchen had described them, and thought about his bedlamp with the night light in the base and his pillow, doing his best to push away the things he really missed.

Given time, he might have gotten used to all of it: the

distance between what he had expected and this place, the fact that everybody was so *old*; the things he was a little homesick for. Trying to close at least part of that distance, he sought out the Pipe Dreams the next morning; they were slouching out of the house in a line, one, two, three in shapeless garments; they could have been dressed for a day in the fields and so he stepped in front of the first of them, saying:

"Hey, the garden, let's go work in the garden."

So that the first old lady saw him, and, her memory fired by the word *garden*, said, "Forget all that work stuff honey, let's just take off all our clothes." Then she reached for him, with the other two clustering, trying to recall certain inner fires, all three so ugly and avid that he leaped away from them, terrified, without time to think about what he was doing, or what he was about to do.

"It's me," he said as soon as he got his mother on the phone, collect. He had more or less rolled down the hill behind the farm and he was at the phone booth in the center of town. "It's me, Mom, Ralph III."

"Baby." Just beyond her voice there were the clicks of the tracing mechanism working. "Baby, where are you?"

"Mommy, come and get me." It all came in on him: the bedlamp, the pillow, pretty things that stayed where you put them, parents who kept track of you. "Oh Mom, I'm at Gretchen's farm and it's just horrible."

Out of the tail of his eye he saw Gretchen getting out of the truck and as he hung up she said. "You called them, didn't you?" He nodded, and, to show he loved her, got into the truck. She said, "If you want to go back home that bad, honey, I'll take you. Just let me go by the house and get my beads."

They were packed for the trip, Gretchen with her pockets bulging, when the helicopters came. Marva was the first out of the farmhouse, running into the clearing calling, "Air, Air, don't you know me, it's your mother, Air," and Police Sergeant Patrick McGillicuddy looked her right in the eye for one cold moment, saying:

"People like me can't afford to know people like you."

"La la," the Pipe Dreams sang, weaving for a new audience: "La la sha na la la la."

One of the cops said, "You'll be a lot better off where you're going."

"My beads," Gretchen said, "I only got half my beads."

"Tell it to the judge."

"Just so long as it's Robertson J. Caldwell of the Second Circuit, he's my baby," Man Superstar said, pushing a bleary face up close to the sergeant's. He went on, but everybody thought he was maundering. "He's my baby Jewel."

At headquarters the bailiff opened his arms to the Pipe Dreams, saying, "Why Ma," but nobody could be sure which one he meant. When the public defender came it was Anne Twelvetrees's boy Tonto, who said he called himself Arnold Zweibaum now and washed his hands of the case. Anne began, "How sharper than a serpent's tooth . . ." but the bailiff pushed her along with the three Pipe Dreams, who were still hugging him, never mind which one he really belonged to. Anne hugged right along with them, thinking at least one of the kids was glad to see them after all these years.

Holding on to both his parents, Biff could hear Gretchen behind him, saying, "Well, Archer, maybe you will be better than Moon was, he kind of went overboard." For reasons neither of them understood at the moment, she had been cut out from the rest of the farmhouse family and stood, handcuffed, next to the desk.

He said, softly, "I guess I thought you were another kid."

"I'm not a kid." She lifted her chin. "I'm a grown-up lady, and hell, honey, what could I expect? You're only a kid."

When he woke the next morning Biff was in his own bed, hugging his own pillow, with his bedlamp glowing softly because his mother had turned on the night light in the base. He could smell breakfast cooking and he thought he heard his father, who had stayed behind in Oregon to attend to some business, and was coming in some time this morning. He had waked up screaming a couple of times so his bedroom door was open now, cracked so his mother could hear him. Instead he heard her:

". . . she'll be more comfortable there."

"She already looks better with some of that godawful hair cut off. You should have seen the collection of beads she had, some of them were awful and some of them were worth quite a bit."

"She was so *dirty*. Oh Ralph, why didn't you tell me before?"

"I guess I was ashamed, you know, partly for having a mother like that, partly for running out on her. The Bissells from in town, they wanted me because they couldn't have any kids of their own and after a while I guess I wanted them." Biff's father was clicking glass against glass: pouring a drink? "It was the nothing regular that got to me, in all those years with Gretch there was nothing regular. I didn't know what was the matter, really, until I got to school and all the other kids had own houses and own rooms and hot meals that they had to get home in time for and after a while it was all I ever wanted, and not all that freedom, all that empty time." There was pain in his voice. "I only wanted to know what was coming next."

"I love you, Ralph," Biff's mother said. "Look at all you've done for her."

By that time Biff was on the bed with his knees up, squinting in remorse because he understood where

Gretch was; he was trying to push his face up with his fists, as if he could push the thoughts up at the same time, so he could get one on top and deal with it.

When he wouldn't stop yelling and breaking things they agreed to let him see his grandmother. The place was clean and cheerful, with lots of people her age and bouncy nurses with red cheeks and squidgy rubber shoes; there were window boxes and construction paper cutouts pinned on the bulletin boards and taped to windows, and her room, when they got to it, was on the sunny corner of the building. Because she hadn't adjusted yet, the room was white, simple and more or less empty of sharp objects. The bed was white and so was the sculptured chair she sat in. She was white too: the dye had been washed out of her hair and the rest of her was scrubbed and her tan had faded. When he went in (alone, because he insisted), she didn't seem to notice; she stared without seeing but he found himself compelled to whisper on and on to her anyway, not able to be sure how he felt about all this, except that she was a nice lady and in spite of the fact he had loved her he had brought her to this; he talked on and on, his words bubbling out in the white room, and when he couldn't think of anything more to say to her he did what he had come for, fishing out the blue beads she had given him and pressing them in her hand, kissing her at the same time and saying, shouting, "Look, Gretchen, look," so that she did look, finally, fixing on them with a sweet smile that made everything a little better. She looked him in the face now, pleased and still smiling, and, cupping the beads in her hands she kissed him and spoke.

"Oh thank you. Thank you, Moon."

The Berkley Showcase

New Writings in Science Fiction and Fantasy
Edited by Victoria Schochet & John Silbersack

Presenting a new kind of series for all science fiction and fantasy fans, highlighting exciting new fiction that will define the direction of both genres for the 1980's. No easy reads. No stale voices from the past. Just the most daring, the most controversial, the most unforgettable science fiction and fantasy you will read. Join us.

_____**THE BERKLEY SHOWCASE: Vol. 1**
04446-7/$1.95

_____**THE BERKLEY SHOWCASE: Vol. 2**
04553-6/$2.25

_____**THE BERKLEY SHOWCASE: Vol. 3**
04697-4/$2.25

_____**THE BERKLEY SHOWCASE: Vol. 4**
04804-7/$2.25

Berkley Book Mailing Service
P.O. Box 690
Rockville Centre, NY 11570

Please send me the above titles. I am enclosing $_____
(Please add 50¢ per copy to cover postage and handling). Send check or money order—no cash or C.O.D.'s. Allow six weeks for delivery.

NAME_____
ADDRESS_____
CITY_____STATE/ZIP_____ 97AU